Disney PRINCESS

Once Upon a Princess

Disney PRESS

New York

Stories translated from the Disney Libri series by Carin McLain

Printed in the United States of America

First Edition

10 9 8 7 6 5 4 3 2 1

ISBN: 1-4231-0498-6

Visit www.disneybooks.com

Table of Contents

THE STORY OF
ARIEL

MONTH OF THE SHELL, FIRST DAY OF THE RED ALGAE

I've decided that starting today I will keep a diary. I want to write down all the thoughts I can't share with anyone. I want to leave a record of my most secret adventures. Of course, I have to have secrets—because if my father ever knew about everything I do . . . Oh, Daddy is a good sea king, and I know he loves me. But he worries much too much about me! He always sends Sebastian along to keep an eye on me and make sure I don't have any fun. Oh, I know Sebastian is Daddy's most trusted adviser, and under that hard shell he's really sort of soft. But he sure can be crabby!

Luckily, I can slip away from him once in a while to visit the surface. And I love writing all about the fantastic things I've seen up there. The human world is so fascinating!

Anyway, Daddy can never, ever know about any of this. He thinks I'm still a little girl, but he's wrong. I'm almost grown up, and the sea just isn't big enough for me anymore. I want to see the whole world. And that includes the human world above the sea. My most secret, exciting, wonderful dream? To meet a real, live human in person and talk to him. That would be the most incredible thing in the world!

I know what Daddy would say about that. He'd say that humans are all barbarians who kill sea creatures every chance they get. But I'm sure not all of them are like that. Daddy is very wise, but he doesn't know everything.

This evening, a little sea horse told me about a sunken ship he saw a few miles from the palace. Tomorrow, Flounder and I are going to check it out. I hope I find lots of interesting human objects to add to the collection in my secret hideaway! I'll just have to make sure I'm home in plenty of time for Daddy's concert. . . .

Oh! I'm so sleepy. Better get to bed now, or I'll be too tired to explore or sing tomorrow. Good night, Diary!

MERMAIDS, SHARKS, AND GUPPIES

"Ariel, wait for me!" Flounder, the little yellow fish gasped as he tried to keep up with the red-haired mermaid swimming ahead of him.

"Flounder, hurry up!" Ariel called, excitedly.

"You know I can't swim that fast!" Flounder cried.

Ariel waited impatiently for her best friend to catch up. "There it is," she said, pointing through the murky waters of the ocean floor at the ruins of a sunken ship ahead. "Isn't it fantastic?"

"Yeah, sure. It-it's great," Flounder stammered. But

he wasn't too sure about that. Being this far from the safety of the palace made him very, very nervous. There could be anything lurking in these deep, open waters. "Now let's get out of here," he added.

"You're not getting cold fins now, are you?" Ariel teased.

"Who, me? No way," Flounder answered, trying to cover up. "It's just that it looks damp in there, and I think I may be coming down with something," he said, suddenly starting to cough.

"All right, I'm going inside," Ariel said as she started swimming toward a porthole. "You just stay here and watch for sharks."

"What? Sharks!" Flounder exclaimed, hurrying after the little mermaid. "Ariel! Wait!"

"Flounder, don't be such a guppy," Ariel said, ignoring his worried comments as the two friends swam through the porthole.

"I am not a guppy!" Flounder cried, insulted. Then, pretending to be as brave and excited about the sunken ship as Ariel herself, he said, chuckling nervously, "This is great, I mean, I really, uh, love this excitement . . . adventure . . . danger lurking around every cor—AAAAAH!" His comment ended in a shriek of fear as he came across the skeleton of a sailor who had gone down with the ship.

Meanwhile, Ariel had already made her way up to a higher deck. She immediately spotted something shiny—a strange metal object with three prongs sticking out of some rotted wood.

"Oh, my gosh!" She exclaimed as she grabbed the item. "Have you ever seen anything so wonderful in your entire life?"

Flounder looked at the metal item curiously. "Wow, cool!" he agreed. "But, uh, what is it?"

"I don't know," Ariel replied, tucking the item into her sack. "But I bet Scuttle will!"

Scuttle was one of Ariel's surface friends. He was a seagull who knew all about the human world. He was always happy to look at the treasures the little mermaid found and tell her what they were (even if he didn't really know himself).

Flounder wasn't thinking about Scuttle just then. Was it his imagination, or had he just heard a deep, threatening rumble from outside the ship?

"What was that?" he asked nervously. "Did you hear something?"

But Ariel wasn't listening. She had just found another weird-looking human object. It was made out of wood, and it had a wide hole at one end and a smaller, flatter hole at the other. She picked it up and stared at it. "Hmm, I wonder what this one is?"

"Ariel!" Flounder was growing more nervous by the second.

Ariel glanced at him. "Flounder, will you relax?" she said. "Nothing is going to happen!"

At that moment, a huge, shadowy shape loomed up right behind the little yellow fish. Flounder screamed in terror. "Aaah! Shark!" he shrieked.

Flounder and Ariel swam for their lives. The giant shark came after them, smashing through the walls of the ship and tracking them around the mast. Finally, Ariel tricked it into swimming right into the metal hoop at the top of the ship's anchor. The shark was trapped!

"You big bully!" Flounder shouted. Then he and Ariel swam quickly away.

A few minutes later, they surfaced near a rocky

island. Scuttle was sunning himself there, but he came right over when he spotted them.

"Scuttle, look what we found!" Ariel exclaimed, holding up her bag.

"We were in this sunken ship, and it was really creepy," Flounder added.

"Human stuff, huh?" the seagull said knowingly. "Let me see."

He dug into the bag. The first thing he pulled out was the metal object.

"Look at this! Wow! This is special. This is very, very unusual," he said, examining the silver fork. "It's a dinglehopper! Humans use these little babies to straighten their hair out." He demonstrated, twisting the pointy parts of the item in the feathers on top of his head. "See? Just a little twirl here, and a yank there—" He finished with a flourish.

Ariel took back the item and stared at it in awe. "A dinglehopper!" she exclaimed.

"What about that one?" Flounder asked, pointing to the second item.

"Ah, this I haven't seen in years. This is wonderful—a banded bulbous snarfblatt," Scuttle announced, picking up the pipe. "Humans invented the snarfblatt to make fine music. Allow me—" He put the snarfblatt to his beak and blew, but all that came out was salt water and seaweed.

Meanwhile, Ariel's face had gone white. "Music!" She gasped. "Oh, the concert!" In all the excitement, it had completely slipped her mind! "Oh, my gosh, my father's going to kill me!" She grabbed her bag. "I'm sorry, I've got to go. Thank you, Scuttle!"

Ariel and Flounder swam back to the palace as fast as they could. But it was too late. The concert was over.

King Triton was very disappointed in his youngest daughter. "I just don't know what we're going to do with you, young lady," he thundered.

Ariel felt terrible. "I'm sorry. I just forgot!"

Triton shook his head. "As a result of your careless behavior—"

"Careless and reckless behavior!" Sebastian the crab interrupted furiously.

"The entire celebration was . . . eh . . ." Triton searched for the right word.

"Well it was ruined!" Sebastian shouted. "Completely destroyed! Thanks to you, I am the laughingstock of the entire kingdom!" Sebastian was the official court composer.

Flounder couldn't stand to hear anymore. "But it wasn't her fault!" he burst out. "First this shark chased us, and then this seagull came, and—"

"Seagull?" Triton repeated.

Flounder knew he'd just made a terrible mistake. He clapped his fins over his mouth, but it was too late. King Triton's face filled with anger.

"You went up to the surface again, didn't you?" he asked Ariel. "Didn't you?"

"Nothing happened!" Ariel protested.

"Oh, Ariel!" Triton grasped his forehead in frustration. "How many times must we go through this? You could have been seen by one of those barbarians, one of those humans!"

"Daddy, they're not barbarians," Ariel protested.

"They're dangerous!" Triton insisted. "Do you think I want to see my youngest daughter snared by some fish eater's hook?"

"I'm sixteen years old!" Ariel cried. "I'm not a child anymore!"

But King Triton would not back down. "As long as you live under *my* ocean, you'll obey *my* rules!" he shouted.

"But if you would just listen," Ariel tried to explain.

"Not another word!" the king yelled. "And I am never, never to hear of you going to the surface again. Is that clear?"

Ariel couldn't answer. She swam away in tears.

MONTH OF THE SHELL, THIRD DAY OF THE RED ALGAE

*I*t stinks being the youngest of seven sisters! Everyone thinks they can tell me what to do. Ever since I missed the concert, Daddy and my sisters keep acting like I kicked a pupfish or something. Oh, how I wish Flounder hadn't told about our visit to the surface. I've never seen Daddy so angry! If he had his way, he'd probably close me up in a clamshell to keep me safe. Or worse yet, he'll invite Talassio back for another visit to talk some sense into me.

Ha! I know Talassio is the son of Prince Cianos, Daddy's friend. And I know he means well. He's just so . . . so . . . boring! He's only eighteen years old—how can he already seem so dull? All he thinks about is finding a wife and settling down. My sisters think he's cute, and I guess they're right in a way. Talassio is tall and blond, with blue eyes and broad shoulders. But all he is to me is a cute young merman who's so boring, he'll put you to sleep.

Maybe he was trying to be serious just to impress me. Well, it didn't work. I told him that I was the youngest daughter, and according to our laws all my sisters have to get married before I can. You should've seen his face! I could just see him with gray hair and wrinkled scales, still waiting for his turn!

After he left, I felt a little guilty for telling a fib. But it was the only way I could get myself off the hook without hurting Talassio's feelings. I believe a little white lie is better than the truth sometimes, if it's for a good reason.

It's the same thing with Daddy, I think. Sometimes it's better that he not know everything I do or think or feel. For

example, right now I'm writing this in my secret hideaway, surrounded by my collection of things from the human world. Flounder is the only other one who knows about this place, but sometimes I wish I could bring Daddy here. Maybe if he could see all of the wonderful things I've collected, he would realize that humans can't be as terrible as he believes they are. Maybe he would start to understand just how much I long to know about the world up there above the surface. . . .

Hmm, I just heard a noise from outside. Could someone have stumbled onto my secret hiding place? Uh-oh—I'd better check! Until later, Diary . . .

THE STORM

"Sebastian!" Ariel cried as she spotted the crab tripping over a shiny hourglass in her secret hideaway.

"Ariel! What are you . . . How could you . . . er," Sebastian sputtered, gesturing around him with his claws. "What is all this?" The king had sent him to keep an eye on Ariel. And now that he'd followed her to this out-of-the-way cavern, he couldn't believe what he was seeing. Human objects! Dozens of them—maybe hundreds! King Triton would have a fit when he heard about it.

"It's just my collection," Ariel replied.

"Oh, I see, your collection," Sebastian said. "If your father knew about this place he'd—"

"You're not going to tell him, are you?" Flounder interrupted.

"Oh, please, Sebastian," Ariel added. "He would never understand!"

Well, she was right about that! Sebastian tried to be reasonable. "Come with me," he told her. "I'll take you home and get you something warm to drink."

At that moment, a shadow passed over the sunfilled entrance at the top of the grotto. Ariel looked up, ignoring Sebastian's words. "What do you suppose . . . ?" she began, already swimming upward.

She shot up quickly toward the surface, leaving Sebastian and Flounder behind. When she popped her head out of the water, she saw a ship.

The sight left her breathless. She had never seen a ship so close before! The humans on board seemed to be having a celebration. Multicolored sparks shot up into the sky, reflected on the calm surface of the water. Ariel could hear the sounds of happy music and festive voices coming from the deck.

Sebastian and Flounder popped up beside her. "Jumping jellyfish!" Sebastian exclaimed in shock when he saw the ship.

Ariel swam closer. Soon she was near enough to grab one of the rails of the deck and pull herself up for a better look. The sailors were too busy laughing, singing, and dancing to see her. But one creature did notice Ariel—a large, furry dog sniffed her  out and came over to give her a friendly lick on the face. Barking wildly, he bounded over to one of the humans.

"Good boy, Max," the human greeted the dog fondly.

When Ariel took a good look at Max's master, she stared in amazement. The young man was tall, dark-haired, and incredibly handsome. She was sure he had to be the most beautiful human she had ever seen!

Just then, another human—an older man, with
white hair—stepped forward and called for silence.
"It is now my honor and privilege to present our
esteemed Prince Eric with a very special, very
expensive, very large birthday present." Smiling, he
brought the handsome young man forward and gestured to a huge object covered by a cloth. "Happy
birthday, Eric!" he cried, pulling off the fabric.

Ariel gasped. It was a life-size statue of the
young man! Prince Eric, she thought, gazing at the

human. It was a lovely name for such a beautiful person. She smiled as the prince thanked the older man, Grimsby, for the gift.

"Of course, I had hoped it would be a wedding present," Grimsby said. "The entire kingdom wants to see you happily settled down with the right girl."

"Oh, she's out there somewhere," Eric replied, perching on the edge of the deck and staring thoughtfully out to sea. "I just haven't found her yet."

"Uh, well, perhaps you haven't been looking hard enough," Grimsby suggested.

Eric chuckled. "Believe me, Grim, when I find her, I'll know. It'll just hit me—like lightning."

At that very moment, a bolt of lightning flashed through the night sky, and the rumble of thunder drowned out the men's voices.

"Hurricane!" one of the sailors cried. "Stand fast! Secure the rigging!"

A strong wind began to blow, thunder rattled, and rain pelted down on the deck. Soon the ship was tossing and turning in gigantic storm-blown waves.

Then a lightning bolt struck the mast—and the ship was in flames! It ran aground on some rocks and started to sink.

Ariel was safe because she could just go beneath the surface, but she was worried about the humans. She watched as they abandoned the ship, jumping into lifeboats. But Eric realized one member of the crew had been left behind.

"Max!" he shouted. He climbed back on board, tossing his beloved dog to safety just seconds before a keg of gunpowder caught fire and the ship exploded.

In the lifeboats, the other humans looked on in horror. They were sure the prince was lost forever!

But Ariel spotted Eric as he clung to a piece of wood. A second later, he lost his grip and sank below the surface.

Ariel dove down and caught him, swimming with all her might until she reached the surface. She didn't know much about humans, but she knew one thing for sure—they couldn't breathe underwater!

It was past dawn by the time Ariel managed to

drag Eric's limp body onto the sandy beach of a deserted cove. The storm had passed, though clouds still dotted the sky overhead.

"Is he—dead?" Ariel asked anxiously, staring down at the human.

Scuttle flew down to help. "It's hard to say," the seagull said thoughtfully, examining Eric's foot for signs of life. "I can't make out a heartbeat."

Just then, the prince's lips parted and he sighed. Ariel gasped. He was alive!

She stared at him. He was so handsome! She

longed to know more about him—what would it be like to know him, to be part of his world? She found herself singing to him in her magical mermaid's voice. She was still singing when his eyes finally opened.

Eric had no idea where he was. Who was the beautiful girl staring down at him? The sun was in his eyes, so he couldn't see her very well. But he could hear her! Her voice was like an angel. . . .

Suddenly, there was a bark and the sound of voices from the edge of the cove. Someone was coming!

Ariel panicked. She couldn't let the other humans find her here. What would they do if they saw her? All her father's warnings flashed through her mind.

Leaving the prince on the beach, she dove below the safety of the waves.

MONTH OF THE SHELL, FIFTH DAY OF THE RED ALGAE

What is happening to me? Diary, if you only knew. Since the first moment I saw Prince Eric, my whole life began to feel different. Part of me wishes I'd stayed with him, there on that beach, even though I wasn't sure what would happen next. But all I could do was watch from a distance as his friend Grimsby found him. Oh, and Max, too, of course.

Thinking about how he risked his own life to save Max makes me shiver. How can someone who would do that be a barbarian? Oh, how I wish Daddy could have

seen it! But I can never tell him. He would be so angry—I can't imagine what he'd do. I'm just happy that Sebastian agreed not to tell. I think he's hoping this is the end of the adventure.

But I can't help wishing it's just the beginning. I can't stop thinking about Eric—my sisters are starting to give me strange looks and muttering about my dreamy eyes and my humming. I can't help myself! What a strange feeling, when Prince Eric's eyes looked into mine. It was as if he knew me—knew me better than anyone else ever has.

But what can I do about it? Eric and I come from different worlds. I live under the water. He lives on land. I have fins, he has legs. What can possibly come of this? I feel so confused. . . . I wish I could talk to my sisters. They're older than me, and they know more about love. But they would only go running to Daddy if they heard I was falling in love with a human.

I know! I'll go talk to my mother's wise old nursemaid, Crystalla. She has always kept all of my deepest secrets and given me advice. I know I can trust her.

I think I'll go right this minute. Until later, Diary . . .

THE SECRET
OF THE SEA WITCH

Crystalla knew everything there was to know about life in the sea, and even quite a bit about life on land. She had lived many, many years in King Triton's palace, caring for the young members of the royal family. She had retired from her official duties before Ariel was born, but still shared her advice and wisdom freely with anyone who asked.

Ariel had always been her favorite of Triton's daughters. Her spirit and energy reminded Crystalla of the late queen. "Hello, sweetheart," she said fondly when Ariel swam in to greet her.

"Hi, Crystalla," Ariel said softly.

Crystalla peered at her. "Is something wrong, Ariel?" It seemed as if the little mermaid had something on her mind.

"Oh, no, Crystalla, everything's fine." Ariel let out a long, deep sigh.

Aha! Now Crystalla understood. She had seen these symptoms many times before. She smiled. "Ariel, my dear, you are in love!"

Ariel gasped. "How did you know?" she exclaimed. "I haven't told a soul! Oh, except Flounder—that little guppy didn't tell, did he?"

Crystalla laughed and stroked Ariel's cheek. "When you have white hair like mine and so many years behind you, you don't need to be told," she said. "I can see it in your eyes, dear child. But don't look so worried—sixteen years old is the perfect age for a mermaid to fall in love."

Ariel gulped. "Yes, but it's not that simple," she said nervously. "You see, um—that is, er . . ."

Suddenly, Ariel wasn't so sure she should tell. What if Crystalla disapproved? What if Crystalla *did* tell Ariel's father?

"What is it?" Crystalla asked. "Sweetheart, you know you can tell me anything, no matter what it is. Your secrets are mine."

Ariel sighed, knowing she had to trust someone. She would burst if she didn't share her news. Oh, Sebastian and Flounder knew, of course. But they couldn't possibly understand what she was feeling. Maybe Crystalla could.

"You're right," Ariel said, trying to keep her voice from trembling. "I *am* in love. With—with a human."

"What?" Crystalla cried, springing from her seat. "A human!" Her smile disappeared, and a strange expression took its place. "I certainly hope your father doesn't know about this!"

Ariel's heart froze. Oh, no! She had been wrong to trust Crystalla. "Please!" she cried desperately. "You can't tell Daddy about this. Please!"

Immediately, Crystalla's face softened. "Oh,

child," she murmured. "I'm sorry. I've frightened you. But don't be alarmed—I won't tell your father. As I promised, your secret is safe with me."

"Oh, thank you!" Ariel sank to the ocean floor in relief. "But why did you look so strange just now?"

Crystalla sighed. "Ah, Ariel," she said in a faraway voice. "It's just that—well, there are things you don't know about me. I was young once, too, and I liked to swim to the surface every once in a while to look around just like you do." She smiled. "Don't look so surprised. The whole kingdom has seen you staring up toward the surface. In any case, one day I spied a human man, the captain of a ship that often sailed over the kingdom."

She was silent for a moment, remembering the past.

"Yes?" Ariel said softly, curious to hear more. "And was your captain handsome?"

"Oh, yes." Crystalla smiled. "The handsomest

man I could imagine. I would have given anything to get close to him, to speak to him. . . . But the laws of the sea forbid it." She shook her head. "Your father was not the one who invented the rule against humans and merpeople mixing, Ariel. Such laws have been in place for many, many years." She sighed. "Unless your prince somehow trades his legs for fins, or you exchange your fins for legs, it's impossible."

Ariel frowned. Even Crystalla didn't seem to want to help her! "Well, fine!" she cried. "Then I'll just have to figure out a way to change my fins into legs!"

Crystalla chuckled. "But that is impossible, dear child," she said. "The only one who could do such a thing—the only one who *would* do such a thing—is Ursula, the sea witch."

"Ursula?" Ariel repeated slowly. "I—I have heard her name, of course. But nobody will tell me who she is or what she's done. They say I'm too young to understand."

"If you're old enough to fall in love, I suppose

you're old enough to hear Ursula's story," Crystalla said thoughtfully. "It begins many years ago, long before you were born, when your father was a young  king with lots of enthusiasm but not much experience. Ursula lived in the palace then—she was a member of your dear mother's court. She was a strange girl, always getting herself into trouble. But nobody could have imagined all the trouble she would cause once she discovered the lure of dark magic."

Ariel's eyes widened. "Dark magic?"

"I'm afraid so." Crystalla shook her head sadly. "You see, Ursula wasn't satisfied with being just one of the many women of your mother's court; she wanted to be Queen of the Sea herself. She had hoped to marry Triton, but your mother captured his heart instead. So Ursula decided she would accuse King Triton of making a pact with the humans."

Ariel gasped. "Daddy?" she cried. "He would never do that! He thinks humans are barbarians."

"Yes," Crystalla agreed. "But Ursula can be very convincing, especially with the help of her magic. Many of the king's citizens started grumbling, saying that it was time for a new ruler."

"Oh, no!" Ariel was horrified. "Then what happened?"

"Fortunately, Sebastian overheard Ursula bragging to her pet eels, Flotsam and Jetsam," Crystalla said. "He told the king—and everybody else—and so

Ursula's plan was discovered before any real damage was done. She was banished from the kingdom forever, and from that day on, she has been known as the sea witch. She swore that sooner or later she would have her revenge on the king. Let's hope that day never comes."

Ariel agreed with that. She was so busy thinking about Crystalla's story that she forgot about her own problems for a little while.

And even when she remembered, she didn't feel quite as confused as she had before. It had helped to talk to someone about Eric—especially since Crystalla had once loved a human herself.

Of course, Crystalla had only admired her captain from afar. Ariel wasn't sure how, or when, but she was determined to do much more than that.

She had to find a way to see Eric again and tell him how she felt.

MONTH OF THE SHELL, FIFTH DAY OF THE RED ALGAE

*T*here is so much to write, and so little time!
Flotsam and Jetsam are waiting for me—I told
them I needed a moment to get ready.

But I should start at the beginning. I was still thinking
about my talk with Crystalla while Sebastian lectured me—
again—on why it was better to stay safely under the sea and
give up thinking about the surface world.

In the middle of it, Flounder pulled me away, saying
he had a big surprise. He led me to my secret hideaway—
and I almost exploded with joy. There was the statue of
Eric! It had fallen into the sea during the shipwreck,

and Flounder had found it and brought it there.

I was so excited I didn't hear Daddy coming until it was too late. I don't know how he found the hideaway, or how he knew about what had happened, but he did. He was furious—especially when I told him I was in love with Eric! Before I could stop him, he raised his trident and destroyed everything . . . even the statue.

My hand shakes as I write about it. I was too upset to think. All I could do as he left was cry.

A moment later, I heard a pair of strange voices:

"Poor child—she has a very serious problem. If only there was something we could do."

Then one of them said, "But there is something."

I looked up and saw two eels swimming around me. "Who are you?" I asked them nervously. There was something about their eyes—I wasn't sure I should trust them.

"Don't be scared," they told me. "We represent someone who can help you—someone who can make all your dreams come true. Just imagine: you and your prince, together forever."

How could they know? "I don't understand," I said.

"Ursula has great powers," they said with a hiss.

At first I was horrified. I remembered the terrible story Crystalla had told me earlier. I couldn't go to the sea witch for help! Not after what she'd done to Daddy.

Daddy . . . I looked around at the ruins of my beautiful collection. Daddy claimed he wanted me to be happy. But he seemed willing to destroy all my chances for true happiness.

Maybe Ursula was the answer, after all. Hadn't Crystalla said that the sea witch was the only one who might be able to change my fins into legs? Surely, it was worth a try. Right?

Well, the eels are still waiting. I don't want them to leave without me. So for now, farewell, Diary. May all my dreams come true before I write here next. . . .

SILENT LOVE

The closer Ariel got to Ursula's lair, the more nervous she felt. The water was getting darker and gloomier. Just outside the sea witch's cave, she saw a horrible sight. Hundreds of small, pitiful sea creatures anchored to the seafloor like limp water plants, with gaping jaws and huge, sad eyes that stared at Ariel as she passed. What were they? Ariel couldn't imagine. She wasn't sure she wanted to know.

Swimming past the imprisoned creatures as quickly as possible, she found herself looking in at a large, purple-skinned, white-haired, half-octopus figure.

"Come in, my child," Ursula greeted her, smiling. "We mustn't lurk in doorways. It's rude. One might question your upbringing." She chuckled. "Now then. You're here because you have a thing for this human, this prince fellow. Not that I blame you. He is quite a catch, isn't he? Well, angelfish," she

continued. "The solution to your problem is simple. The only way to get what you want is to give up your tail and become a human yourself."

Ariel gasped. Ursula had read her mind! "Can you do that?" she asked.

Ursula smiled. She could tell that the little mermaid had already made up her mind. It would be easy to reel her in—hook, line, and sinker. And that was just what the sea witch wanted. Sealing one of her sly magical deals with Triton's daughter would give her just the revenge she'd been looking for all these years!

"My dear, sweet child," Ursula said, assuringly, "that's what I do. It's what I live for, to help unfortunate merfolk like yourself—poor souls with no one else to turn to."

Then the sea witch laid out her terms. "Now, here's the deal," she said. "I will make you a potion that will turn you into a human for three days. Before the sun sets on the third day, you've got to get dear old Princie to fall in love with you. That is,

he's got to kiss you," the witch explained. "Not just any kiss—the kiss of true love. If he does kiss you before the sun sets on the third day, you'll remain human permanently."

Ursula waited until she saw Ariel's smile of joy. Oh, yes—hook, line, and sinker.

"But, if he doesn't," Ursula continued, "you turn back into a mermaid. And you belong to me. Have we got a deal?"

Ariel thought about what she had just heard. It sounded wonderful—she was sure Eric felt the same way she did. She had seen it in his eyes that day on the beach. They could be together forever!

Then she thought of something else. "If I become human, I'll never be with my father or sisters again."

"Life's full of tough choices," Ursula commented. "Oh, and there is one more thing—we haven't discussed the subject of payment. You can't get something for nothing, you know."

"But I don't have anything!" Ariel cried.

"I'm not asking much—just your voice," Ursula said.

"My voice?" Ariel put a hand to her throat, surprised. Without her voice, how could she explain things to Eric, tell him who she was? True, he had looked into her eyes—but he had just awakened from unconsciousness. There was no guarantee he would recognize her face. "But without my voice, how can I—?" she began.

The sea witch interrupted, already knowing what the little mermaid was thinking. "You'll have your looks and your pretty face," she assured her. Then she waved her hand and a scroll appeared, outlining the deal.

Ariel thought about

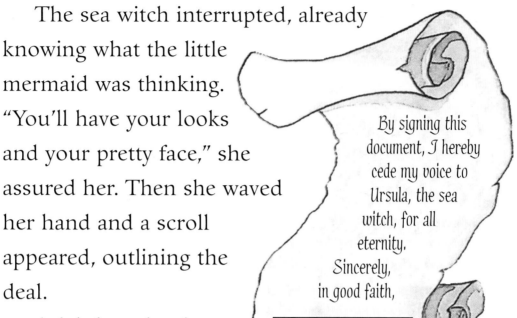

By signing this document, I hereby cede my voice to Ursula, the sea witch, for all eternity.
Sincerely,
in good faith,
_____

her father, her sisters, her home under the sea. Then she thought about Eric—about the possibility of never seeing him again.

That made up her mind. Taking the fish-bone pen Ursula offered, she signed her name at the bottom of the scroll. The ocean churned as Ursula captured Ariel's voice inside a magical shell and turned her tail to legs.

FIRST STEPS

Ariel was overwhelmed with so many feelings. First, of course, there were her new legs. They were so amazing, so wonderful! They weren't quite as easy to work as her familiar old tail, though. It took her a while to get the hang of standing upright on them without toppling over.

Then there were her friends. Oh, she had expected Scuttle to offer his help. And she knew that Flounder would be faithful, no matter what. But she hadn't been sure what Sebastian would do.

As soon as Ursula had mixed up her potion and

cast her spell, Ariel had suddenly discovered that she couldn't breathe underwater anymore. She'd choked and gasped, struggling to take a breath.

Luckily, Flounder and Sebastian were watching from the doorway. The two of them had rushed her up to the surface just in the nick of time. Then they had carried her to the same beach where she had taken the human prince. Scuttle had found them there and helped Ariel make a human-style dress out of an old abandoned sail. Flounder even dove down to retrieve Ariel's diary so she would have a way to record her adventures on land.

But Sebastian was worried and angry about what Ariel had done. At first he'd threatened to rush off and tell the sea king right away. He'd muttered something about finding Ursula and reversing the spell.

But then he'd seen Ariel's face. He

knew that if he went to the king now, she would be completely miserable for the rest of her life. Instead, he reluctantly offered to come along and help her if he could.

"What a soft shell I'm turning out to be," he muttered as she kissed him in thanks.

Another strange thing to get used to was not having a voice. She had to communicate with her friends with nods and smiles.

But she didn't care. It was worth it to be with Eric!

The sound of excited barking erupted from nearby. It was Max! He came running toward the cove.

Scuttle flew off, Flounder dived under the water, and Sebastian hopped inside a fold in Ariel's dress. Ariel was nervous as the dog bounded up to her.

Then Max greeted her with a big, slobbery lick— just as he had done back on the ship. He remembered her! Ariel was happy. Maybe Eric would remember her, too, and she wouldn't have to worry about not being able to explain. . . .

Just then, she heard a familiar voice shouting Max's name. It was Eric! He hurried down the beach, following Max's barks. He seemed startled to see Ariel sitting on a rock.

"Oh! Are you okay, miss?" he asked with concern. "I'm sorry if this knucklehead scared you. He's harmless really." He ruffled the dog's fur fondly, then peered at Ariel more closely. "You seem very familiar to me. Have we met?"

Ariel nodded eagerly. He remembered her!

"We have met! I knew it! You're the one I've been looking for!" he cried, grasping her hands as Max barked happily. "What's your name?"

Ariel opened her mouth to answer. Then she remembered—she couldn't speak. She put her hand to her throat, dismayed. She gestured, trying to make Eric understand.

It only took him a moment to catch on. "You can't speak?" His voice filled with disappointment. "Oh, then you couldn't be who I thought you were."

Ariel was disappointed, too. How could he not recognize her? She had thought that her eyes could reveal to the prince what her mouth could not express.

Nevertheless, she tried not to lose heart. There was still time.

MONTH OF THE SHELL, FIFTH DAY OF THE RED ALGAE

*O*h, how I've wished for this day! I have seen such wonderful things today—met so many wonderful people. Now that I'm unable to speak, I feel the need to write more than ever. I'm so grateful to Flounder for rescuing you, dear Diary!

Even though Eric doesn't know who I am, he has been so kind to me. He brought me back to his castle, where some maids helped me wash up and change into real human clothes. It feels so strange, all this cloth against my brand-new legs! Strange, but nice.

I was a little worried when I realized Sebastian had

disappeared along with the dress Scuttle made me. But he turned up at dinner, safe and sound.

Speaking of dinner, I had a few embarrassing moments at the table, thanks to Scuttle's mistakes. It turns out that dinglehoppers aren't for fixing one's hair—humans call them "forks" and use them to eat with. And when I saw Grimsby holding a snarfblatt, I blew into it, hoping to make music. Instead, black dust flew out, making a mess— it was really a pipe!

But Eric laughed in such a nice way that I didn't mind

my mistakes. He makes me feel so comfortable! Every moment I'm with him, I'm more certain than ever that I did the right thing. I only wish Daddy could understand. . . .

But no, I can't think about him right now. I need to fall asleep. Tomorrow, Eric promised to take me on a tour of the kingdom. That means the two of us will be alone together all day. That will be my chance to get Eric to kiss me! I'm a little nervous, but I know I can do it.

So now, time for bed. I'm sure all my dreams will be sweet ones!

KISS THE GIRL

Early the next morning, Ariel sat beside Eric in his carriage, ready for the marvelous sights that awaited her.

Everything was so new to her! To start with, Eric's carriage was pulled by a horse—a huge, wonderful creature that was nothing like a sea horse at all. The town square was filled with so many interesting things that she hardly knew where to look first.

And the music! Now that she had legs, it seemed

she could hardly stop dancing. As a band of musicians played, she dragged Eric out for a dance.

After that, they drove out of the village into the countryside. Eric even let Ariel drive the carriage for a while.

Finally, as the sun began to set, the two of them set out in a rowboat on a peaceful lagoon. The evening songs of crickets and frogs accompanied them as they floated along. As he rowed, Eric was overcome with an almost irresistible urge to kiss the red-haired girl sitting across from him.

But that was silly. He hardly knew her! Besides, his heart belonged to another—the mysterious girl with the beautiful voice who had rescued him from the shipwreck.

To take his mind off his thoughts, he spoke to the girl. "You know, I feel really bad about not knowing your name," he told her. "Maybe I can guess." He thought for a second, guessing the first name that came to him. "Is it, uh—Mildred?"

He could tell that he was wrong right away by the look on her face. He laughed. It was amazing how much this girl could communicate without ever saying a word!

"How about Diana? Rachel?" he continued to guess.

Suddenly, as if spoken by a little voice out of nowhere, a name popped into his head—*"Ariel."*

"Ariel?" he said uncertainly. He had never heard that name before.

At the name, the girl's eyes lit up. She smiled and nodded happily, grabbing his hands.

"Ariel," he repeated, a little amazed that he'd managed to guess. Of course, he didn't have any idea that a little crab named Sebastian had just whispered the name into his ear! "That's kind of pretty," Eric went on.

He and Ariel smiled at each other as the boat floated on. Now that he knew her name, Eric felt closer to this girl than ever. Once again, he was gripped by the urge to let her know how he was feeling. He leaned toward Ariel, about to kiss her when . . .

SPLASH! Without warning, the boat overturned, dumping them both into the shallow water. That was the end of the romantic moment.

Ariel could hardly hide her disappointment. Why did this have to happen now, just when all her dreams were about to come true?

She didn't see Flotsam and Jetsam, Ursula's two eels, grinning with satisfaction and swimming away. They had capsized the rowboat. They knew that the sea witch didn't want Ariel to succeed. If she did, all of Ursula's plans for revenge would be ruined!

Back at the castle, Ariel stood on the balcony outside her room. She looked at the moon shining down on the sea and thought about the day she had just shared with Eric. Even though it made her feel sad to be away from her family and friends, she couldn't help feeling happy. She and Eric were becoming closer and closer. He hadn't kissed her yet, but she still had another whole day.

And she planned to make the most of it.

A Surprising Announcement

The next morning, Ariel was awakened by Scuttle's excited voice. He flapped in through the open window, calling her name.

"Ariel, wake up! I just heard the news!" he cried. "Congratulations, kiddo—we did it!"

As the little mermaid opened her eyes and looked at the seagull sleepily, Sebastian yawned and rubbed his eyes. "What is this idiot babbling about?" he grumbled.

"The whole town's buzzing about the prince getting himself hitched this afternoon!"

For a moment, Ariel wasn't sure what to think. Married? Eric was getting married? But then she realized what Scuttle meant. Eric wanted to marry *her!*

She smiled and spun around the room gleefully. After that almost-kiss yesterday, Ariel had thought she would have to work harder to convince Eric that she was the one for him. But he had figured it out on his own!

Not even taking the time to get dressed, she raced out of the room and down the stairs. She had never been so happy in all her life.

MONTH OF THE SHELL, SIXTH DAY OF THE RED ALGAE

I hadn't even made it down the steps when I saw him . . . when I saw them. Eric—my Eric—was arm in arm with a beautiful girl with long, dark hair. At first, I didn't understand. Then I heard Grimsby saying something about how he was mistaken, that Eric's mystery maiden from the beach really did exist.

But how could this be? I was the girl from the beach! Surely, Eric had to realize that by now. . . .

But no. I heard him say that he and this other girl, Vanessa, were to be married—today! Their wedding ship would depart at sunset.

I could feel my heart breaking. Just when all my dreams seemed about to come true, all hope was lost!

I came here to the beach to write down my thoughts and figure out what to do. But what can I do except stare out at the sea I left behind? I've never felt so lonely or hopeless in all my—

Ariel stopped writing in midsentence. Was she seeing things, or was that a merperson emerging from the waves? She gasped.

It was Crystalla! She couldn't believe the old nursemaid would defy King Triton's orders.

But sure enough, it was her old friend. "Oh, my child!" Crystalla exclaimed as Ariel raced into the shallow water to hug her. "Flounder just told me everything. You must come with me—perhaps together we can change the sea witch's mind."

Ariel looked puzzled. For a moment, she wasn't sure what Crystalla meant.

"Hurry—before the sun sets and your time runs out," Crystalla urged. "We still have a few hours. I know things about Ursula that you can't even imagine. If there's a way to convince her to return you to your old form, we'll find it."

Now Ariel understood. Was it possible? Could Crystalla convince Ursula to turn Ariel back into a mermaid?

But wouldn't that be like admitting she'd been wrong to try? Ariel glanced at the castle behind her. It hadn't been wrong. Maybe the wrong thing would be to give up now, to go back on her vow to see this through.

Ariel shook her head no. She needed to do this on her own. She hugged Crystally tightly.

Leaving Crystalla behind, Ariel headed back toward the castle.

VANESSA

As the afternoon wore on, the wedding ship was prepared for its evening cruise. While the castle's staff bustled around the bride, Ariel watched from a distance.

How had it happened? How had the mysterious Vanessa managed to steal her true love's heart in just one day?

She wished she could talk to Prince Eric, to try to explain. Her voice! Why had she given up her voice?

She glanced at the diary in her lap. For once, she

hadn't wanted to write about her feelings. She hadn't written one word since that morning.

But maybe writing was the answer. Maybe she could write down her true identity, her story, and show it to Eric!

But no. Her shoulders slumped as she realized that wouldn't work. Even if she could find Eric and convince him to read such a thing on his wedding day, he would only laugh. A mute girl who combs her hair with a fork and says she's a mermaid—it was too crazy.

Besides, he was in love with someone else.

Soon the ship was ready. Ariel was invited to the wedding, but she hid behind a pillar as the wedding party boarded the boat and the sailors pulled up the anchor. She couldn't bear to watch Eric marry someone else. She would just wait here until sunset, when the sea witch arrived to claim her prize.

As the wedding ship sailed out of the port, Ariel sat crying on the dock. Sebastian and Flounder were

with her, but neither could think of a single thing to say to make their friend feel better.

Suddenly, a terrible squawk interrupted the sad scene. It was Scuttle. He had just peeked in a window of the wedding ship and seen Vanessa getting ready for the ceremony. But when she'd looked in the mirror, Scuttle had seen her true face reflected in the glass—it was the sea witch! She had disguised herself as a beautiful human girl and used Ariel's captive voice, which she held in a locket around her neck, to win Prince Eric's heart! And it had worked—the prince had thought Vanessa was the girl from the beach who had saved him.

"What are we going to do?" Flounder exclaimed.

Ariel didn't waste a moment. It was almost sunset. In a few minutes, it would be too late. Ursula would have her soul—and Eric, too. She couldn't let that happen!

She raced across the dock and dove into the sea, forgetting for a moment that she couldn't swim as easily now with legs as with her tail. Sebastian came to

her rescue, rolling a large barrel into the water. Ariel grabbed it, and Flounder pulled the barrel toward the ship.

 "I've got to get to the sea king," Sebastian muttered anxiously. "He must know about this!"

"What about me?" Scuttle asked, wondering what he could do to help.

"Find a way to stall that wedding!" Sebastian cried as he leaped into the water.

Scuttle took his orders seriously. He roused every bird, fish, lobster, and seal he could find and led them to the ship. The ceremony had already begun, and Scuttle wasted no time. He and a gang of birds dive-bombed the bride and groom. Sea creatures leaped on board from every direction, splashing the guests. Soon the entire ship was in chaos!

Meanwhile, Flounder was struggling to pull the barrel that Ariel was leaning on. Ariel knew he was trying his best, but her heart pounded nervously as she looked at the setting sun. It was halfway below the horizon. She would never make it in time!

But she was wrong. They finally reached the ship, and Ariel climbed on board. She was greeted by a scene of total mayhem. Scuttle and some of the other creatures were chasing Vanessa.

Vanessa screamed as Scuttle pulled at the shell necklace containing Ariel's voice. The string snapped and the shell tumbled to the deck, where it broke into dozens of pieces. There was a flash of

light, and the sound of sweet singing. Freed from its magical prison, Ariel's voice floated up until it found its true home in Ariel's own throat.

The little mermaid began to sing.

"Ariel?" Eric said uncertainly when he heard that haunting, familiar song coming from the red-haired girl.

"Eric!" Ariel cried happily. Now, at last, she would be able to explain! It seemed too good to be true!

It was at that moment, just as Eric bent to kiss Ariel at last, that the sun dipped below the horizon. It was too late!

Still disguised as Vanessa, Ursula laughed in victory as Ariel slipped from Eric's arms. Ariel fell to the deck as her legs transformed back into a tail. Then, Ursula changed back into her true form and grabbed Ariel. The wedding guests gasped in horror and fear.

"So long, lover boy!" the sea witch called out to Eric as she threw herself into the sea, dragging Ariel with her.

A Terrible Trade

As they sped toward the bottom of the sea, King Triton appeared before them. "Ursula! Stop!" he shouted. "Let her go!"

"Not a chance, Triton. She's mine now," Ursula retorted. "We made a deal."

The sea witch unfurled the scroll that Ariel had signed. Such a contract couldn't be broken by anyone, not even the sea king.

"But I might be willing to make an exchange," Ursula said. She offered Ariel's soul in exchange for Triton's own—along with the trident that would

make Ursula the queen of the sea at last.

Ariel looked on in horror as her father raised his trident. He wouldn't—he couldn't! But a second later, it was done. He signed his own name on the scroll over Ariel's. Ursula cackled in triumph as the powerful King Triton shrank down, down, down until he had become one of those pitiful little sea creatures like those outside Ursula's cave.

"Your Majesty!" Sebastian said sadly.

"Daddy!" Ariel cried. She couldn't believe her

father had made such a sacrifice for her. For the second time that day, she felt as if her heart was breaking.

"At last it's mine!" Ursula exclaimed as she picked up Triton's crown and trident.

Suddenly, something sliced through the water. It was a harpoon! Ursula cried out in fury as she turned and saw Prince Eric swimming behind her. He had followed her deep into the ocean, determined to save his beloved Ariel.

"Eric, look out!" Ariel cried.

"After him!" Ursula shouted at Flotsam and Jetsam.

"Say good-bye to your sweetheart," Ursula told Ariel as she aimed the trident at Eric.

But Ariel wasn't ready to say good-bye just yet. Instead, she grabbed Ursula's hair. The trident's bolt shot off-course. Instead of hitting Eric, it struck the two eels, destroying them!

Now Ursula was *really* furious. Gripping the trident, she called on all her magic powers. She grew larger and larger until she was twice the size of Eric's ship. Ariel and Eric, clinging to each other, looked on in horror.

The sea churned around them as Ursula whipped up the surface of the water with her enormous tentacles, raising waves as high as mountains. Suddenly, a gigantic whirlpool arose from the bottom of the sea. As Ariel got sucked into it, the sea witch aimed the trident at the little mermaid, shooting bolt after bolt at her. Ariel dodged the first few, but she knew it was only a matter of time until the sea witch destroyed her.

But Eric hadn't given up. The whirlpool had brought the wreck of his old ship to the surface. Climbing aboard, he spun the rudder until the sharp remnant of the ship's broken mast was aiming straight at the sea witch. By the time Ursula turned to see what was coming, it was too late.

The terrifying scream of the sea witch echoed throughout the undersea kingdom. She fell with a mighty splash. A moment later, the sea closed over her forever.

HAPPILY EVER AFTER

It was all over. The end of the sea witch meant an end to all of her dark magic. As the trident sank to the ocean floor, King Triton regained his true form. So did all the other souls of the poor sea creatures Ursula had imprisoned over the years.

But even though she'd helped defeat the terrible sea witch, Ariel couldn't feel completely happy. Perched on a rock, she watched Eric, who

was lying exhausted on the shore.

Ursula had been defeated. But nothing else had changed. Ariel was still a mermaid, and Eric was still a man. Would they now have to live the rest of their lives apart, despite all that had happened?

Suddenly, there was a magical golden flash. Her fins tingled, and to her amazement, she saw them turning back into legs!

She turned and saw her father smiling at her, holding his trident. Of course! His good magic was

much more powerful than Ursula's dark magic had
ever been. And finally, he had
used it to give her the
one thing she had
always wanted.
Maybe he did
understand,
after all!

MONTH OF THE SEA HORSE, SECOND DAY OF THE SEA STAR

*T*he next time I write, I'll use the human calendar, but for now I want to enjoy the things that remind me of my old home under the sea. Now that I no longer feel myself a prisoner there, I find I can remember that world with love.

I can hardly believe Eric and I are married! We just held the ceremony here on this ship so that Daddy and the rest of my undersea family and friends could be part of it. I've never been so happy!

Still, it's sad to say good-bye to everyone. Of course,

I'll still be able to see them sometimes on the beach. But it won't be the same.

A little while ago, Crystalla came to say good-bye. We found a quiet spot off the side of the ship. Our relationship has always been special, so I wanted our good-bye to be special, too.

That's when she gave me her wedding gift—a pair of earrings made of the whitest, most precious pearls from under the sea. She told me they'd once belonged to my mother. It was the most wonderful gift I could imagine—I couldn't help crying a little. But they weren't really tears of sadness. They were tears of joy for having such wonderful friends in my life—both on land and under the sea.

I'll never forget the world that I come from. But I'm ready to start my life in a new world—Eric's world, the wonderful, amazing world of humans, which is about to become my world, too.

I guess sometimes dreams really do come true!

THE STORY OF
Jasmine

A Golden Cage

Once upon a time, in a faraway land, there was a city called Agrabah. It was a place of mystery and enchantment. Narrow streets and twisted alleyways ran past houses of all shapes and sizes. Most of them led to the marketplace, where it was possible to find almost anything for sale—fresh figs, woven baskets, colorful silks, and much more. People from all over the kingdom gathered there, and the sounds of bargaining, shouting, and laughter filled the air.

The Sultan's palace overlooked it all. Although it

had a fine view of Agrabah, the palace was separated from the city's smells, sounds, and people by high walls. Nobody could go in or out without passing the Sultan's guards.

Inside that palace lived Princess Jasmine, the daughter of the Sultan. Jasmine was beautiful and spirited, with long, raven-colored hair and curious brown eyes. She had everything her father's riches could buy—mouthwatering foods, beautiful clothes, many loyal servants. Yet she was not happy. . . .

One sunny afternoon, three days before her sixteenth birthday, Princess Jasmine sat beside a fountain in the palace garden. Her pet tiger, Rajah, had just chased away another prince who had come to seek her hand in marriage. Her father, the Sultan, was very upset.

The Sultan loved his daughter. He wanted her to choose a suitor because it was the law—Princess Jasmine had to be married to a prince by her sixteenth birthday. But he also wanted her to find a husband so she would have someone to take care of her.

But Jasmine didn't see what the big hurry was. "If I *do* marry, I want it to be for love," she told her father. "Please try to understand—I've never done a thing on my own. I've never had any real friends!"

At that, Rajah looked up in surprise, and Jasmine laughed.

"Except you, Rajah," she assured the tiger with a pat. Then she turned to her father again, hoping he would understand this time. "I've never even been outside the palace walls!"

The Sultan was shocked. "But, Jasmine, you're a princess!" he exclaimed. Princesses didn't just wander around outside. Agrabah could be dangerous. Why couldn't Jasmine see that?

Jasmine frowned. "Then maybe I don't want to be a princess anymore!" she cried.

"Oooh!" The Sultan clenched his fists. Why did she have to be so stubborn about this? "Allah forbid *you* should have any daughters!" he cried, throwing his hands in the air.

Jasmine sighed and skimmed her fingers across the surface of the water in the fountain as her father stormed away. He just didn't understand. All he thought about was that stupid law.

"The law is wrong!" Jasmine murmured as she

stared at her reflection in the fountain.

She sighed again. If only her mother were still

alive, maybe she would

 understand. But she had

died when Jasmine

was a baby. Jasmine

only knew her

mother's face from

the framed picture

she carried with her

everywhere she went.

Everyone said that Jasmine looked just like her
mother. Jasmine only wished she'd had a chance to
know her. Instead, she had been raised by kind and
caring nursemaids and other servants. She loved
them all—especially her most faithful and dear old
nursemaid, Amina—but it just wasn't the same.

Jasmine had tried many times to explain her feelings to her father, but it was hopeless. He didn't
seem to understand his daughter at all. Nobody did.
Sometimes Jasmine felt just as trapped as the doves

who lived in the elegant aviary just
beyond the fountain. Like the doves,
she lived in a golden cage—she could
see the outside world, but she wasn't allowed to
experience it.

A sudden impulse overtook her,
and she jumped to her feet and
approached the aviary. She stared at the
birds. They were well fed and cared for by the palace
staff. But was that enough for them? Did they long
to soar into the blue sky overhead—the sky they
could see through the bars of their beautiful golden
prison?

She opened the door on the
side of the cage. The doves
hesitated for a moment,
cooing uncertainly. Then,
in a burst of white, they
exploded out of the
aviary and soared into
the fresh open air.

Jasmine followed the white cloud of birds with her gaze until they were lost in the distance.

Finally, the princess was smiling.

Meanwhile, in the throne room, the Sultan was still trying to figure out why his daughter was so upset. Why didn't she want to get married? It was the way things were done!

"I don't know where she gets it from. Her mother wasn't nearly so picky. . . ." he grumbled to himself.

At that moment, the Sultan's grand vizier entered the room. The Sultan smiled when he saw him.

"Ah, Jafar!" he cried. "My most trusted adviser. I am in desperate need of your wisdom."

Jafar bowed to the Sultan with a smug smile. "My life is but to serve you, my lord," he said.

"It's this suitor business," the Sultan explained with a sigh. He had discussed the problem with Jafar many times before. "Jasmine refuses to choose a husband. I'm at my wit's end!"

Jafar was prepared for this moment. "Now then . . . perhaps I can divine a solution to this thorny problem," he said. "But it would require the use of the Mystic Blue Diamond." He fixed his gaze on the enormous aqua-colored stone on the Sultan's finger.

The Sultan gasped in surprise. "My ring?" he said, glancing down at the stone. "But . . . it's been in the family for years."

Once again, Jafar was prepared. He lifted his cobra-headed staff. Its red eyes began to glow.

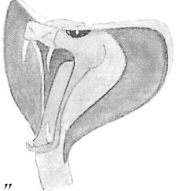

"Don't worry," Jafar said soothingly. "Everything will be fine."

The Sultan stared into the cobra's eyes. His eyes began to glaze over. Soon he was completely hypnotized by Jafar's magic.

Jafar smiled in triumph as the Sultan handed over his ring. Now that he had the Mystic Blue Diamond, Jafar would finally be able to locate the

treasure he'd been seeking for years—a treasure
hidden deep within the legendary Cave of

Wonders.

Many had sought the gold,
jewels, and other riches that lay
within the cave. But Jafar was not interested in those
things. The only thing that interested him was a
common lamp, similar to those that
could be found in homes all over
the kingdom. But the lamp was much
more than what it seemed. It was not the humble
outside that mattered, but what was within.

The trouble was that the Cave of Wonders was
guarded by a fierce tiger-spirit. Jafar had tried to
enter the cave once before with the help of a petty
thief named Gazeem. But the tiger-spirit's voice had
boomed, "Only one may enter here—one whose
worth lies far within: a diamond in the rough."

When Gazeem stepped forward into the cave, the
tiger's mouth instantly closed up and the cave
disappeared into the sand. Apparently, Gazeem was

not the diamond in the rough. But with the help of the Mystic Blue Diamond, Jafar was determined to find the one who could enter the cave and use him to get what he wanted.

Once inside Jafar's secret laboratory, he and his parrot, Iago, brought out a magical hourglass, which held the all-seeing "sands of time." By activating the Mystic Blue Diamond's powers, the sands parted in the hourglass, revealing to Jafar the diamond in the rough—a boy in the Agrabah marketplace.

Outside in the garden, Jasmine was still thinking about her own problems. As she stared at her reflection in the fountain, she pictured her father in the water. She knew he wanted what was best for her. But he didn't seem to understand what she truly wanted.

What was she going to do? She couldn't stay here and marry one of the pompous, boring princes who came to call. And yet she didn't seem to have any other choice. Or did she . . . ?

An Adventure Fit for a Princess

I have to get out of here! Jasmine thought as she walked through the palace gardens. She looked around at the familiar sights. She knew every path, every tree, every blossom in the flower beds. The palace and these gardens had made up her entire world. Until now . . .

"Princess! Princess Jasmine!"

It was the servants calling her  name—probably so they could help her dress for dinner. But instead of walking toward the voices, Jasmine hurried in the opposite direction.

Soon the princess reached the palace kitchens, which lay near the gate where the servants and other workers entered and exited the palace. She paused and glanced longingly at the heavy wooden doors built into the smooth walls. If only she could simply open those doors and walk outside. . . .

But she knew that was impossible. The doors were guarded at every moment, day and night. She would never be able to escape that way.

However, she had a different plan in mind. Every day, women from the marketplace arrived, carrying large baskets of food—luscious fruits, crisp vegetables, sweet dates, fresh fish—that they wanted to sell to the palace cooks. Jasmine hid behind a shrub and waited, knowing that another market woman would be arriving soon. Sure enough, a woman soon arrived at the gates. She was dressed in a plain brown cloak and carrying a basket of figs. Jasmine waited until the woman passed close by her hiding place. Then she reached out and pulled her behind the shrub.

The woman cried out in terror. "Allah save me!" she exclaimed fearfully.

"Don't be frightened!" Jasmine whispered, shushing her. "I won't hurt you. I only ask a favor."

The woman stared at her. "Who are you, beautiful lady?" she asked. "What do you want of me?"

For once, Jasmine was glad that almost no one in the kingdom had ever seen her except at a great distance. She didn't want the woman to know that she was really the princess.

"My name doesn't matter," she said. "Only my request. Please, I beg of you—may I have your cloak?"

The woman seemed surprised at the request. "My—my cloak?" she said, pulling it a bit tighter around her. "But why? Your garments are much finer."

"Yes, but I really need your cloak," Jasmine said. "It's very important."

Still the woman hesitated. "I would surely help you if I could, fine lady. But I have no other cloak besides this one."

Jasmine knew that if she revealed her identity as the princess, the woman would hand over the cloak without question. But she didn't want to do that. The whole point of this adventure was to escape her life as a princess.

Instead, she slipped the ring she was wearing off

her finger. "Please," she said, holding it out to the woman, "take this in exchange. You can sell it and buy yourself a new cloak."

The woman gaped at the beautiful stone set in the ring. She had never seen such a fine jewel. Surely, it would buy her a thousand new cloaks, made of silk and fine linen.

Reaching out with trembling fingers, the woman touched the ring. "But I couldn't," she whispered. "It's worth so much more than my simple cloak."

"I know." Jasmine smiled at the woman's honesty. She pressed the ring into her hand. "But, please, I beg of you, accept the trade."

When the woman looked into Jasmine's eyes, she saw desperation there—perhaps her humble cloak really was worth more than jewels to the pretty young lady. Setting down her basket of figs, the woman quickly slipped off the cloak.

Many hours later, just as dawn's first rays touched the horizon, a figure wrapped in a plain brown cloak slipped through the palace gardens.

The figure paused beside a tall tree growing next to the high garden wall. When the figure looked up, the cloak's hood fell back. It was Jasmine.

She reached up her hands to climb the tree. Just then, she felt a tug on the hem of the cloak. It was Rajah.

Jasmine smiled sadly at her friend. "I'm sorry, Rajah," she said, "but I can't stay here and have my life lived for me. I'll miss you!"

She hugged the tiger. Then Rajah stood beside the wall to help her up the first few feet to the tree. He watched sadly as she climbed to the top of the wall.

Pausing, she glanced back for one more look at the gardens—and one more smile for her old friend. She blew Rajah a kiss. "Good-bye!"

Moments later, Jasmine found herself wandering through unfamiliar streets. At first, things were quiet. But as morning arrived, Agrabah came to life.

Jasmine wasn't sure where to look first. There were interesting sights to see everywhere she

turned! Then she reached the marketplace, and found even more new sights, sounds, and smells.

She saw sword swallowers, fire breathers, snake charmers, and even a fakir who could lie for hours on a bed of nails. As she walked around, the street vendors tried to sell her everything under the sun.

"A pretty necklace for a pretty lady!" one man crooned as she passed his stall. Jasmine smiled politely and kept on walking.

Even more fascinating than the goods in the market stalls were the people who were milling about—so many people! Jasmine had known only the servants and the residents of the palace. She didn't know anything about the rest of her father's subjects. As she passed a fruit stand, she saw a little boy. His big eyes were fixed on a basket of juicy apples.

Jasmine stopped and smiled at the little boy. "Oh,

you must be hungry," she said, picking up the plumpest, juiciest-looking apple and handing it to him. "Here you go."

All of a sudden, a gruff voice from behind her yelled, "You'd better be able to pay for that!"

Startled, Jasmine turned and saw a large, rough-looking man scowling at her. "Pay?" she whispered, suddenly remembering that she wasn't in the palace anymore. Out here, nobody knew that she was the princess.

"No one steals from my cart!" the fruit seller exclaimed angrily.

"I'm sorry, sir," Jasmine said, feeling frightened for the first time since scaling the palace wall. "I don't have any money."

"Thief!" the man shouted.

Jasmine backed away, realizing she'd made a big mistake. "Please, if you let me go to the palace, I can get some from the Sultan. . . ."

The man grabbed her by the wrist. "Do you know what the penalty is for stealing?" he cried, lifting his sword.

Jasmine froze in terror. How had she gotten herself into this mess?

She almost closed her eyes as the man's sword started down toward her. But at the last moment, a hand shot out and stopped it.

"Thank you, kind sir!" a new voice cried out happily. "I'm so glad you found her!" A dark-haired boy with sparkling eyes was standing there. He looked at Jasmine. "I've been looking for you."

Jasmine blinked. What was going on? She had never seen this boy before in her life—yet he acted as if he knew her. "What are you doing?" she whispered to him uncertainly.

He winked. "Just play along," he whispered back.

Meanwhile, the fruit seller had lowered his sword, looking confused. "You know this girl?" he asked the boy.

The boy shrugged. "Sadly, yes. She is my sister." He leaned closer and twirled one finger beside his head. "She's a little crazy."

Jasmine frowned for a moment, insulted. But then she realized that this must be part of the boy's plan.

"She said she knew the Sultan," the fruit seller said suspiciously.

"She thinks the monkey is the Sultan," the boy replied, pointing to the pet monkey sitting on his shoulder.

Jasmine decided she'd better play along, as the boy had said. "Oh, wise Sultan!" she cried, bowing before the little monkey. "How may I serve you?"

Out of the corner of her eye, she saw the boy secretly swipe an apple from another pile. He handed it to the fruit seller, pretending it was the apple Jasmine had given to the little boy. Then he grabbed Jasmine by the arm.

"Come along, sis," he said. "Time to see the doctor."

Jasmine was starting to have fun with this game.

"Oh, hello, doctor. How are you?" she said, smiling at a nearby camel before the boy dragged her away to make their escape.

A few minutes later, the boy, the monkey, and Jasmine were climbing stairs in an abandoned building. The boy, whose name was Aladdin, was used to making narrow escapes through the alleyways of Agrabah. He was curious about the girl he'd rescued. She wasn't from around here—he lived on the streets and knew almost everybody. Who was she? Where had she come from?

But first they had to reach the safety of his hideout. He helped the girl climb over fallen stones and loose boards. But when it was time to leap over an alleyway between two rooftops, she refused his help. Grabbing a pole, she vaulted over the alley herself.

Aladdin smiled, impressed with the stranger's

spirit. He could already tell she wasn't like any girl he'd ever met before.

Finally, they reached Aladdin's hideout on the roof of an abandoned house. "Is this where you live?" the girl asked, looking around curiously.

"Yep! Just me and Abu," Aladdin replied, gesturing to the monkey. "We come and go as we please."

"That sounds fabulous," the girl said with a sigh.

Aladdin was surprised—he liked his home, but it was far from fancy. "So where are you from?" he asked.

"What does it matter?" Jasmine replied, staring toward the palace in the distance. "I ran away, and I am *not* going back."

"Why not?" Aladdin asked.

"My father is forcing me to get married," Jasmine explained.

Aladdin gulped. Married? For some reason, the idea of this girl getting married disturbed him.

Meanwhile, Jasmine was wondering what had come over her. How could she sit here, telling all her most private secrets to a stranger? Still, there was something about the boy that made her want to trust him. . . .

"May Allah grant you his protection on this day, Princess Jas—"

Amina's words broke off with a gasp. The princess's loyal servant had just drawn back the curtains on Jasmine's royal bed to reveal that it was empty!

"What is it?" A young handmaiden heard the older woman's gasp and came to see what was wrong. "Oh, no!"

Soon every maid in the palace was searching for the missing princess. But she was nowhere to be found. With a heavy heart, Amina went in search of the Sultan to give him the terrible news.

Instead, she found Jafar just outside the throne room. "What is it, woman?" the vizier snarled impatiently.

Amina trembled as she bowed. All the servants were afraid of Jafar's foul temper and sneaky ways. "It's the princess, sir," she whispered. "This morning, I entered her chamber as usual, but. . . ."

She went on to explain. As she spoke, Jafar stroked his beard thoughtfully. The princess missing? Interesting. Perhaps he could use this to distract the Sultan from other matters—such as wondering what Jafar was really doing with the Mystic Blue Diamond. He would have to save this news for a time when it best served him. . . . He realized the servant woman was still speaking.

". . . And so, I was about to inform the Sultan of the terrible news," she whispered timidly, bowing again.

"Never mind," Jafar told her firmly. "I shall inform his lordship myself. Do not worry yourself about it anymore. The princess shall be found."

Amina was surprised at the vizier's mild response. She had been expecting him to throw her in the palace dungeon for delivering such terrible news. "Yes, sir," she said with a final bow. "Thank you, sir." With that, she scurried away.

Jafar entered the throne room, where the Sultan was sitting on his throne, worrying over Jasmine's marriage.

"Oh, hello, Jafar." The Sultan greeted his adviser, distracted by his worries. "Everything all right in the palace this morning?"

"But of course, sire," Jafar said to him smoothly. "Everything is fine. Just fine."

CAPTURED!

As Jasmine and Aladdin gazed at the view of the faraway palace, there was a shout from the stairway leading to the rooftop. It was the palace guards!

Jasmine and Aladdin both jumped to their feet. "They're after me!" the two of them cried at once.

Then they stared at each other in surprise. "They're after *you*?" they said at the same time.

But there was no time to discuss it. So they ran. But the palace guards were everywhere! Soon there was no place left to run.

Aladdin looked over the edge of the roof. Maybe there was a way. . . .

"Do you trust me?" he asked.

Jasmine stared at him. "What?"

"Do you trust me?" Aladdin repeated.

Jasmine looked into his eyes. She could see something in them—something honest and true. "Yes," she said.

He took her hand, and they jumped. Seconds later, Aladdin, Jasmine, and Abu landed safely in a soft pile of milled grain. The three of them leaped up and started racing through the marketplace.

But Rasoul, the head palace guard, and his men didn't give up. Jafar had ordered them to find Aladdin—the Mystic Blue Diamond had revealed him to be the only person who could enter the Cave of Wonders.

"We just keep running into each other, don't we, street rat?" Rasoul sneered as he grabbed Aladdin. "It's the dungeon for you, boy!"

Aladdin shouted for Jasmine to run. But she stepped forward, furious at the way the guards were manhandling her new friend. Her father would never approve of such behavior!

"Let him go!" she demanded.

Rasoul laughed, not recognizing her. "Looky here, men!" he cried. "A street mouse!"

"Unhand him! By order of the princess!" Jasmine let the hood of her cloak fall to her shoulders, revealing her face.

"Princess Jasmine!" Rasoul exclaimed, shocked. Immediately, he and the other guards bowed in respect.

"The princess?" Aladdin said as his jaw dropped open in amazement.

"What are you doing outside the palace? And with this street rat . . .?" Rasoul continued.

"That's not your concern. Do as I command. Release him!" Jasmine ordered.

"I would, Princess," Rasoul said apologetically. "Except my orders come from Jafar. You'll have to take it up with him."

Jasmine's eyes narrowed. She should have
known Jafar was behind this outrage! "Believe me,
I will!" she cried.

Now that she had been seen, Jasmine knew her
adventure was over. She didn't have time to worry
about that, though. She was too concerned about
what might become of her new friend at the hands
of the palace guards. She had heard stories from the
servants of the terrible things that sometimes went
on in the palace dungeons.

Rasoul and several of his guards dragged Aladdin
away. Others stayed behind to accompany the
princess. As she passed a group of children playing
in the street, she felt a tug on her cloak. She turned
and saw the little boy she had given the apple to a
little while before.

"Thank you, miss," he responded shyly.

"Why, hello again," she said with a smile.
"What's your name?"

"Kerim," the boy answered. "Why are those
guards following you? Did you steal another apple?"

"No." Jasmine laughed. "They're accompanying me to the palace."

"The palace!" The boy's eyes widened. "Do you live there? Have you ever seen the princess? They say she is very beautiful."

"Yes, I've seen her many times," Jasmine answered truthfully, hiding a smile. "Maybe you'll see her yourself one day."

"Oh!" The boy looked amazed at the idea.

Jasmine then realized that Rasoul and his prisoner were out of sight. She had to speak with Jafar before anything terrible happened to her friend. "I have to go now, Kerim. But one day I'll take you to the palace to meet the princess. I promise."

With a wave to the little boy, she hurried on her way, with the other guards in tow.

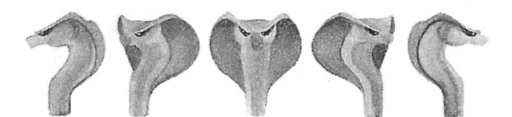

Back at the palace, Jasmine quickly located the grand vizier. She glared at him as he bowed to her. Although Jafar was her father's closest adviser, Jasmine didn't trust him one bit.

"Princess," he greeted her. "How may I be of service to you?"

"The guards just took a boy from the market— on your orders," she snapped.

Jafar shrugged, seemingly surprised at her anger. "Your father has charged me with keeping peace in Agrabah," he said. "The boy was a criminal."

"What was his crime?" Jasmine demanded.

Once again, Jafar feigned surprise. "Why, kidnapping the princess, of course," he purred. He was pleased with the way things had worked out. Jasmine's escape had given him the perfect excuse to snatch Aladdin without anyone's complaining— not even that ridiculous softy of a sultan.

Jasmine gasped in horror. "He didn't kidnap me!" she cried. "I ran away!"

"Oh, dear, how frightfully upsetting," Jafar lied.

"Had I but known . . . the boy's sentence has already been carried out."

"What sentence?" Jasmine asked fearfully.

"Death," Jafar replied. "By beheading."

Jasmine felt her knees go weak. That poor boy—this was all her fault!

"How could you?" she whispered to Jafar. Then she turned and ran away, sobbing.

A few minutes later, she sat at the edge of the fountain in the palace gardens. Rajah gazed at her somberly.

"It's all my fault, Rajah," Jasmine said, hugging the tiger for comfort. She couldn't believe that the wonderful, lively, caring boy she had met was gone forever. And all because he had tried to help her.

"I didn't even know his name," she whispered.

PRINCE ALI

"Jafar, this is an outrage!" the Sultan cried. Jasmine had come to him, terribly upset, babbling something about a boy and a beheading and the grand vizier. After a while, he'd managed to figure out what it was she was sobbing about. "If it weren't for all your years of loyal service . . . but from now on, you're to discuss sentencing of prisoners with me—*before* they are beheaded!"

"I assure you, Your Highness, it won't happen again," Jafar replied.

The Sultan sighed with relief. Good—then, that

was settled. "Jasmine, Jafar," he said, taking one of each of their hands and bringing them together. "Now, let's put this whole messy business behind us."

"My most abject and humblest apologies to you as well, Princess," Jafar said to Jasmine.

Jasmine scowled in return. "At least some good will come of my being forced to marry," she declared. "When I am queen, I will have the power to get rid of *you*!"

With that, she turned and stormed away. How

dare Jafar think a simple apology would make up for what he had done? Yes, the sooner he was gone from the palace, the better. Of course, that didn't make her much happier about being forced to marry a man she didn't love. . . .

As she thought about that, there was a sudden commotion from outside the palace walls. Curious, Jasmine stepped out on the balcony of her quarters.

There was an enormous procession making its way through the streets of the city, headed toward the royal palace. At the front of the parade was a group of dancers in splendid, bejeweled attire. Next came an imposing regiment of armed guards followed by dozens of glamorously dressed servants and a menagerie of exotic animals. Musicians played trumpets, drums, tambourines, and flutes. An elephant draped in beautiful silks carried a magnificent canopied seat on its back. Upon the seat, a handsome young man dressed in white waved to the crowds that had gathered to see him pass.

"Make way for Prince Ali Ababwa!" someone shouted.

Another suitor, Jasmine thought with a sigh— does he really think he can win my heart with such a spectacle?

She had seen enough. Spinning on her heel, she went back inside. But she could still hear the music and the shouts of the spectators.

After a moment, her curiosity got the better of her. What would her father think of this latest suitor? After all, her birthday was only two days from now. . . .

Jasmine crept toward the throne room, listening to the muffled voices coming from within. She could hear her father giggling, sounding delighted, and Jafar muttering, sounding annoyed. She also heard a third voice—a strangely familiar one.

She peered into the room. Her father was clapping his hands happily. "Jasmine will like this one!" he cried.

Prince Ali Ababwa smiled. "And I'm pretty sure I'll like Princess Jasmine."

Jasmine frowned. No, the voice wasn't familiar, after all. She had never in her life heard anyone sound so pompous. She entered the throne room, but the trio didn't notice her.

"Your Highness, no," Jafar put in. "I must intercede—on Jasmine's behalf. This boy is no different from the others. What makes him think he is worthy of the princess?"

"Your Majesty, I am Prince Ali Ababwa!" the young man responded. "Just let her meet me! I will win your daughter."

This was too much! "How dare you!" Jasmine cried. "All of you! I am not a prize to be won!" Before the startled men could respond, she turned and stormed out.

Later that evening, Jasmine sat in her room, wondering if she would ever be happy again. It was a beautiful night, clear and warm, with countless stars twinkling in the sky overhead. But Jasmine was in no mood to appreciate their beauty. Even Rajah's company couldn't cheer her up.

"Princess Jasmine." A voice reached her ears. It came from the balcony.

Jasmine blinked in surprise. Nobody could get to her balcony without passing through this very room. "Who's there?" she called suspiciously.

"It's me, Prince Ali Ababwa."

Jasmine frowned. However he had reached the balcony, she wasn't interested. "I do not want to see you," she retorted.

Rajah loped out toward the balcony. A moment later, Jasmine heard the prince babbling in fear. She smiled and went to the doorway to watch.

The young man had his turban in his hand, trying to shoo the huge tiger away. Without his turban, he looked . . . different. Almost familiar. Jasmine gazed at him thoughtfully.

"Wait," she said. "Do I know you? You remind me of someone I met in the marketplace."

"The marketplace?" Prince Ali repeated, quickly placing the turban back on his head. "Ha! I have servants who go to the marketplace for me. Why, I even have servants who go to the marketplace for my servants. So, it couldn't have been me you met."

Jasmine sighed. She should have known it was wishful thinking that had made this stuck-up prince look so much like that boy she had met. "No, I guess not," she murmured.

Meanwhile, the prince was giving her a nervous smile. "Um, Princess Jasmine," he said. "You're very . . . punctual."

Jasmine wondered if she had heard him right. "Punctual?"

"Uh—uh—beautiful!" the prince corrected quickly.

Jasmine sighed. All the other suitors had said the same thing. "I'm rich, too," she said, giving in to the temptation to tease him a little. "The daughter of a sultan."

"I know," Prince Ali said eagerly.

"A fine prize for any prince to marry," Jasmine went on.

"Uh, right," Prince Ali agreed uncertainly. "A prince like me."

Jasmine had had enough of this game. "Right—a

prince like you," she snapped. "And every other stuffed shirt, swaggering peacock I've met!" She waved a hand dismissively, suddenly wishing he would just disappear. "Just—jump off a balcony!"

"Uh, you're right," Prince Ali said quietly. "You aren't just some prize to be won. You should be free to make your own choice. I'll go now."

With that, he stepped off the edge of the balcony. Jasmine gasped. It was many stories to the hard ground below. He would be killed!

"No!" she cried.

"What?" he said, stopping . . . in midair!

"How are you doing that?" she asked, perplexed. She stepped forward as the prince floated upward. He was standing on a carpet!

"It's a magic carpet," he explained. "You don't want to go for a ride, do you?"

Jasmine hesitated. A magic carpet? She had heard stories of such things. And it would mean another chance to leave the confines of her golden cage. . . .

"Is it safe?" she asked uncertainly.

"Sure," Prince Ali replied. "Do you trust me?" he asked, offering his hand. She stared at him in amazement. Hadn't she already lived this moment?

"Yes!" she whispered, taking his hand.

The stars shone like diamonds as Jasmine settled down on the Magic Carpet. Prince Ali sat beside her. And then they were off!

The Magic Carpet swooped up, up, up, high into the warm night air. Jasmine hardly knew where to look first as they sped over the city. Below, she could see the winding, twisting streets; the crowded, colorful stalls of the marketplace; and the lights of the palace shining over it all.

Then they were leaving Agrabah. The carpet carried them over the desert, where caravans moved

slowly over the sand, and
herds of wild horses ran
free. They passed over
rivers, pyramids, cities, and oceans. Finally, they set-
tled onto the roof of a strange building in a strange,
far-off land. Below, in a square, people wearing
dragon costumes danced and shouted. To Jasmine's
amazement, colorful lights started
exploding in the sky overhead—
fireworks! She had never seen so
many wonders in her life. She had
never even imagined them!

"It's all so magical!" she exclaimed, leaning
against Prince Ali's shoulder.

When she turned to look into his eyes, she saw
something there—something warm, and true, and very,
very familiar. Suddenly, she knew how she could find
out if she was imagining things or not. . . .

"It's a shame Abu had to miss this," she commented casually.

The prince shrugged. "Nah, he hates fireworks.

He doesn't really like flying, either." Suddenly realizing what he'd said, he gulped. "Uh, um—oh, no!"

"You *are* the boy from the market!" Jasmine cried. "I knew it. Why did you lie to me? Who are you? Tell me the truth!"

"The truth?" Prince Ali looked nervous. "The truth is, I sometimes dress as a commoner to escape the pressures of palace life. But I really am a prince."

Jasmine's anger had already passed. She knew about those pressures herself—all too well. "Why didn't you just tell me?" she asked.

"Well, you know . . . royalty going out into the city in disguise—it sounds a little strange, don't you think?"

"Not *that* strange," Jasmine said. Suddenly tired of arguing, she leaned against him. So what if he had kept a secret? It didn't matter. He had told the truth now.

When the fireworks ended, the two of them climbed back onto the Magic Carpet and flew home. Jasmine couldn't remember the last time she had felt so happy.

Prince Ali brought her back to the balcony, helping her step down from the carpet. "Good night, my handsome prince," she said softly.

"Sleep well, Princess," Prince Ali replied, pulling  her toward him for a sweet, good-night kiss.

THE MAGIC OF LOVE

"Oh, Rajah, it was such a wonderful night!" Jasmine cried as soon as she reached her room, with the warmth of Prince Ali's kiss still on her lips.

She sat down before her mirror and picked up a brush. As she brushed her hair, humming the love song Prince Ali had sang to her on their Magic Carpet ride, she thought back over every incredible moment of the evening with the prince. Prince Ali—her friend, her true love, her husband-to-be. Just a day before, she never would have believed

that everything could work out so perfectly.

Jasmine was beside herself with joy. Now she could fulfill her father's wishes, obey the law, and marry a prince by her sixteenth birthday. Prince Ali had arrived just in time to make everyone's dreams come true! Jasmine still could hardly believe how lucky she was. She had to be the luckiest—and happiest—girl in all of Agrabah. In fact, she was sure she had to be the happiest girl in all the world!

Her only regret was that her mother couldn't be there to share in her joy. If only she were still alive . . .

Jasmine wandered to the window and gazed up at the twinkling stars. "Oh, Mother," she whispered. "If you can hear me somehow, hear this. I'm in love! Your little girl has found true love at last. And with Prince Ali by my side, nothing will ever be able to make me unhappy again. . . ."

But there were a few things that Jasmine didn't know about her handsome prince. She didn't know that he was really the street rat Aladdin. He had only become a prince with the help of a genie in a magic lamp!

For Jafar had never had any intention of beheading the young man his guards had taken prisoner. At least, not until Aladdin had served his purpose . . .

 Appearing to the boy as an old beggar, Jafar had helped Aladdin escape from the dungeon and find the Cave of Wonders. Once there, the old man had ordered Aladdin to find the lamp and bring it to him. After that, all the other treasures of the cave would be Jafar's for the taking.

Aladdin had agreed to the plan. Maybe if he discovered a cave full of untold riches, he could prove himself worthy of the beautiful princess who had stolen his heart! But his monkey companion couldn't stop himself from grabbing an enormous jewel. And as soon as Abu's paw touched it, the tiger-spirit awoke from its slumber. The walls of the cave had begun to quake, and the piles of gold coins melted into an endless flow of molten lava.

The only thing that had saved them was the Magic Carpet. It had whisked them through the inferno to the mouth of the cave where Jafar was waiting for the lamp. Suddenly, the cave's mouth had slammed shut, trapping  Aladdin, Abu, and the Magic Carpet inside.

Luckily, Abu still had the lamp! He gave it to Aladdin who rubbed it, trying to read the inscription on its side. Seconds later, a huge, jolly blue genie had burst out of the lamp and offered Aladdin three wishes!

As soon as the Genie had used his magical powers to get everyone out of the cave, Aladdin had chosen his first wish: to become a prince so that he could woo the Sultan's daughter. And so the Genie had transformed him into Prince Ali Ababwa. . . .

Jasmine was still caught up in the magical evening she had shared with Prince Ali when her father arrived at her chamber. She smiled when she saw him, rushing to give him a hug. "Oh, Father! I am so happy!" she said, greeting him.

"You should be, Jasmine," the Sultan replied. "I have chosen a husband for you."

"What?" Her smile disappeared. For the first time, she noticed that the Sultan's eyes looked glazed and far away.

"You will marry Jafar," the Sultan went on.

Jasmine gasped in horror. What was her father talking about? She had chosen her suitor!

The grand vizier and his parrot, Iago, had followed the Sultan into the room. "You're speechless, I see," he said with a cruel laugh. "A fine quality in a wife."

"I'll never agree to marry you!" Jasmine cried. "Father, I choose Prince Ali!"

"Prince Ali

left," the grand vizier said with a wicked smile. He had ordered his guards to knock the boy unconscious and toss him into the deep sea.

"Better check your crystal ball again, Jafar," a new voice interrupted.

"Prince Ali!" Jasmine exclaimed in relief.

Aladdin was furious. It was only the Genie's magic that had saved him from Jafar's dastardly plans. Now, he meant to take care of the evil vizier once and for all. "Tell them the truth, Jafar," Aladdin demanded. "You tried to have me killed."

"What ridiculous nonsense," Jafar said, chuckling nervously.

"Your Highness," Aladdin said, striding toward Jafar and the Sultan, "Jafar has been controlling you with this." He grabbed the cobra staff and smashed it to the ground.

The Sultan immediately came out of his trance. "What?" he sputtered in confusion. "Jafar? You traitor!"

He called for the guards, but Jafar was too quick for him. "This is not done yet," the vizier vowed, disappearing in a cloud of smoke.

Aladdin hurried toward the princess. "Jasmine, are you all right?"

"Oh, yes!" Jasmine cried. The two of them embraced.

The Sultan was still muttering about Jafar's treachery. But suddenly, he noticed what was going on. "What? Can this be true?" he exclaimed. "My daughter has finally chosen a suitor? Ha-ha!" The Sultan was thrilled. "You two will be wed at once. And you'll be happy and prosperous, and then you, my boy, will become Sultan!"

He kept babbling on in his happiness, but Jasmine wasn't really paying attention anymore. She was too busy imagining the wonderful, blissful future that lay ahead.

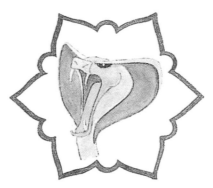

JAFAR'S TRIUMPH

"Try this one, Princess." Amina stepped forward, holding out a soft bundle of purple cloth. Jasmine took it, noting the fine quality of the silk.

"It's beautiful, Amina!" she exclaimed.

Hurrying over to her dressing area, Jasmine quickly slipped on the gown. It fit perfectly, of course—the palace tailors had been working feverishly all night. Jasmine spun around in a circle, admiring the way the folds of the skirt danced around her legs.

"Here, this was made to match." Amina handed the princess a headpiece. The large blue gemstone on it was a twin to the one on the waistband of the gown.

Jasmine carefully fixed the headpiece in place. She smiled at her nursemaid. "Oh, Amina," she said with a sigh. "How can one girl be so happy?"

Amina returned the smile. "No princess ever deserved happiness so much as you, Your Highness," she said kindly. "I knew on the day that you were born that you would be special. I'm so glad your prince has seen that, too."

"Prince Ali is the special one." Jasmine smiled, imagining what the prince would say when he saw her in this dress. Should she save it for the wedding ceremony later, or wear it now to hear her father officially announce his daughter's engagement?

Suddenly, she realized that it was time for the announcement. That made up her mind—she would wear the dress now.

Since the earliest hours of the morning, rumors of the upcoming royal wedding had been flying throughout Agrabah. Guests from neighboring kingdoms were already on their way, and the city had adorned itself for the festivities—banners, flags, and flowers were everywhere, and the air was filled with joyful music. An immense crowd had gathered in front of the palace, eager to get a look at the young groom who would one day be their sultan.

That same morning, Jasmine had sent two of her handmaidens to an alley near the marketplace to find the little house where Kerim lived. The princess had not forgotten the promise she'd made to her little friend—young Kerim and his family would be honored guests at her wedding to Prince Ali.

But for now, Jasmine's thoughts were not of Kerim, but of her handsome prince. She hadn't seen Prince Ali all morning—and the time for the announcement was here! Where could he be?

"People of Agrabah!" her father began from a balcony overlooking the town square. "My daughter has finally chosen a suitor!"

As he went on, Jasmine heard another voice, much closer. "Jasmine?"

"Prince Ali!" she cried, spinning around. "Where have you been?"

"Jasmine, there's something I have to tell you," Prince Ali began.

Jasmine was too excited to pay attention to what he was saying. "The whole kingdom has turned out for Father's announcement!" she cried.

"No, but Jasmine, listen to me, please . . . you don't understand. . . ." Prince Ali said desperately.

Was he getting stage fright at the idea of stepping out before the whole kingdom? Jasmine decided it was better not to give him too much time to worry about it. Besides, her father had just announced the prince's name.

"Good luck!" she whispered, pushing him out onto the balcony.

Nearby, Jafar was watching the celebration, too. The moment he was waiting for had arrived. With an evil gleam in his eyes, he picked up a humble-looking lamp. His sidekick, Iago, had

stolen it from under Aladdin's pillow without the boy's knowing. Now, Jafar would have his revenge!

He rubbed the lamp. The Genie emerged, expecting to see Aladdin, who still had one wish remaining. He gulped in surprise as Jafar laughed triumphantly. "I am your master now!" the vizier cried. "Genie, grant me my first wish: I wish to rule on high—as sultan!"

The Genie was horrified, but he had no choice. It was his duty to obey. Summoning up his magical powers, he stripped away the Sultan's crown, his jewels, even his royal clothes. The poor Sultan was standing there in only his underwear! Seconds later, Jafar had taken his place as ruler of the kingdom. Jasmine could only watch helplessly, while Prince Ali stared at the Genie in horror. "Genie, no!" he exclaimed.

The Genie's big blue face was mournful. "Sorry, kid," he said. "I've got a new master now."

It didn't take long for the Sultan to realize what was happening. "Jafar, you vile betrayer!" he cried.

Jafar smiled. "Finally, you will bow to me," he said with a hiss.

"We will never bow to you!" Jasmine cried defiantly.

Jafar seethed with anger. How dare she? "If you won't bow to a sultan," he said, "then you will cower before a sorcerer! Genie—my second wish. I wish to be the most powerful sorcerer in the world!"

Once again, the Genie had no choice but to do his bidding. Soon Jafar was a mighty sorcerer. He forced the Sultan and Jasmine to their knees with his magic powers. When Rajah tried to stop him, Jafar transformed the tiger into a helpless kitten. But still, Jafar had more tricks up his sleeve.

"Oh, Princess," he said slyly. "There's someone I'm dying to introduce you to."

With that, he changed Prince Ali back into plain old Aladdin. "He's nothing more than a worthless, lying street rat!"

"Ali!" the princess cried in shock as she realized her prince wasn't a prince at all.

"Or should we say—Aladdin?" Iago said,

revealing the boy's real name to Jasmine for the first time.

Before Aladdin could explain, Jafar had flung him into a high tower. Then the sorcerer sent the tower flying up and away—until it landed in an icy land far from Agrabah.

As she watched the tower disappear, Jasmine felt all her hopes for happiness vanish along with it.

THE ULTIMATE POWER

Jasmine couldn't believe what was happening. She watched helplessly as the evil Jafar changed her father into a puppet dressed in a silly jester outfit. He continuously teased and bullied the poor Sultan. It was too much for Jasmine to bear.

"Stop it!" Jasmine cried. "Jafar, leave him alone!"

"It pains me to see you reduced to this, Jasmine," Jafar said, pulling the princess closer to him by the iron chains he had shackled around her. The princess could tell that it angered Jafar that she wouldn't surrender to his power. The angrier he got,

 the more it gave her resolve. She would show him that it took more than magical power to defeat her!

The only thing that made it difficult to go on was thinking about Ali—Aladdin—whatever his real name was. She had thought he was her handsome prince. Now that she knew he was really a street rat, did it change the way she felt about him? Her heart told her no. She thought back to the hideaway on the roof of that old abandoned house, then to the incredible Magic Carpet ride among the stars. Both had been special, because she'd shared them with the one she loved.

She was disappointed that Aladdin had lied to her, but she was starting to understand the reason why he had done so. And remembering his words as she had pushed him out on the balcony to be introduced to the people of Agrabah, she was certain he had been about to tell her the truth at last—even though he would have risked losing her. And that only made her love him all the more.

As Jafar forced the former Sultan to dance for his amusement, Amina crept up to Jasmine's side. "Princess," she whispered, "are you all right?"

"Oh, Amina!" Jasmine's eyes filled with tears. "None of us are all right as long as Jafar is in charge."

Amina stroked her shoulder. "Take courage, Princess," she whispered. "I have an idea. That dented old lamp—it is what gives the evil one his power, yes?"

"Yes, that's right," Jasmine said, glancing at the lamp, which was nestled on a cushion at Jafar's side. "We need to get that lamp away from him."

Amina nodded and smiled slyly.

Jasmine gazed at the maid curiously. "Amina, what are you thinking?" she asked.

"I will save you, Princess," Amina said. "If you will distract the evil one for but a moment, I will be able to take the lamp and bring it to you. Then you will have the power to defeat him!"

Jasmine gasped. "Amina, no! I can't let you do that," she said. "It's far too dangerous. What if Jafar sees you?"

Amina tried to protest, but Jasmine wouldn't listen. She had made up her mind. Jafar had already destroyed one of her loved ones—she wouldn't let him take another.

Amina crept away. Jasmine thought the maid had given up on her crazy plan. But a moment later, Iago pointed to the back of Jafar's chair, where a humble figure was cowering. "You, there—what do you think you're doing?"

With a gasp, Jasmine recognized the figure as Amina. Oh, no! Jasmine's heart sank as she realized her friend had put her own life at risk for her.

"No!" the princess cried as Jafar stood and raised his magic staff. "It's not her fault. It was all my idea!"

"Take her away!" Jafar ordered coldly pointing to the frightened Amina. "She will pay for her betrayal when I've decided upon a fitting punishment."

Guards grabbed Amina and dragged her off. Jasmine watched her go, helpless to do anything to save her friend. When would this nightmare end?

Meanwhile, Jafar's attention had returned to the princess. He forced her to feed him an apple and offer him sips of wine as she grimaced with shame. "A beautiful desert bloom such as yourself should be on the arm of the most powerful man in the world," Jafar said. With his dark eyes glittering madly, he held out a delicate crown of gold.

"Never!" Jasmine cried, throwing the rest of the wine in Jafar's face.

Jafar growled angrily. He was about to strike her when he had a better idea. "Genie," he said, "I have decided to make my final wish: I wish for Princess Jasmine to fall desperately in love with me!" Jasmine gasped in horror. But to her surprise, nothing happened.

That was because the Genie's powers had certain limits—he couldn't kill anyone, raise anyone from the dead, or cause anyone to fall in love with someone else. But Jafar didn't know that.

As Jasmine wondered what would happen next, her eyes suddenly widened with shock. She had just spotted Aladdin at the window!

Though Jasmine didn't know it, Aladdin, with the help of Abu and the Magic Carpet, had narrowly escaped from the cold mountain where the tower had landed. Now, he was back to try to save Agrabah—and the girl he loved.

Jasmine's heart filled with joy, but that feeling was soon replaced by terror. What if Jafar spotted Aladdin now? It would all be over.

She decided the only thing to do was distract him. "Jafar," she said in a soft, beguiling voice. "I never realized how incredibly handsome you are." Slowly, she placed Jafar's elegant gold crown on her head.

The Genie stared in shock, knowing that his

magic had had nothing to do with this odd transformation. But Jafar seemed pleased.

"That's better," he said with satisfaction. "Now, pussycat, tell me more about myself."

Jasmine wanted to shudder with disgust as he smiled at her. Instead, she forced herself to move toward him. "You're tall," she purred, "dark, well dressed. . . ." She was running out of words, so she started praising his eyebrows, his beard, and everything else she could think of. "You've stolen my heart," she finished.

"And the street rat?" Jafar asked.

Jasmine forced herself to keep her gaze on the vizier. But out of the corner of her eye, she could see Aladdin sneaking up toward the lamp.

"What street rat?" she replied smoothly.

Suddenly, Iago, who was struggling with Abu a few feet away, knocked over a fruit bowl. Jafar began to turn toward the sound and—Aladdin!

Seeing what was happening, Jasmine acted fast. She grabbed Jafar—and kissed him.

It was the most horrible thing she had ever had to do. Worse yet, it didn't work. Jafar pulled away and spotted Aladdin and his friends. "You!" he bellowed. "How many times do I have to kill you, boy?"

Before Jasmine knew what was happening, Jafar had trapped her in a giant hourglass. He also turned Abu into a toy monkey, and unraveled the Magic Carpet into a pile of threads. Now, Aladdin had to face the vizier's wrath alone.

"Aladdin!" Jasmine cried desperately.

All she could do was watch as Jafar sent guards, enchanted swords, and everything else he could muster up after the street rat. "Are you afraid to fight me yourself, you cowardly snake?" Aladdin shouted as he dodged Jafar's magical forces.

Jafar laughed, then transformed himself into a huge monstrous cobra. He wrapped Aladdin in his coils. "You little fool," Jafar said with a hiss. "You thought you could defeat the most powerful being on earth? Without the Genie, boy, you're nothing!"

Jasmine pounded against the glass, but it seemed hopeless. The sands of the hourglass were pouring down, burying her alive. Outside, she saw Jafar's coils tightening around Aladdin.

"The Genie!" Aladdin shouted suddenly. "The Genie has more power than you'll ever have. He gave you your power. He could take it away. Face it, Jafar. You're still just second-best."

Jafar hesitated. He had never looked at it that way before. "You're right," he murmured uncertainly. "His power does exceed my own . . . but not for long!" His evil snake eyes flashed with cunning as he realized that since Jasmine hadn't fallen in love with him, he had one more wish left. "Slave!"

he howled at the Genie, who was cowering nearby. "I make my third wish: I wish to be—an all-powerful genie!"

Jasmine was horrified. Aladdin had just given Jafar the ultimate power! How could anybody hope to stop him now?

As Jafar changed form again, this time from cobra to genie, Aladdin slipped free of his grasp. Grabbing a staff, he broke the hourglass, setting Jasmine free seconds before the sand had buried her completely.

Gasping for breath, Jasmine looked up at Jafar. He had become an awe-inspiring red genie.

"The power!" he cried. "The absolute power!"

"What have you done?" Jasmine asked Aladdin sadly.

Instead of looking worried, Aladdin smiled. "Trust me," he murmured. Then he stood and called out to Jafar. "Aren't you forgetting something?" he said. "You wanted to be a genie—you got it. And everything that goes with it."

At that moment, heavy iron chains appeared, clamping firmly onto Jafar's wrists. He stared in horror. An evil-looking black lamp appeared. Jafar felt himself being sucked toward it. He howled in protest, grabbing at Iago to try to stop himself. But seconds later, Jafar disappeared into the lamp.

The Genie rushed over to Aladdin. "Al, you little genius, you!" he cried.

Meanwhile, now that Jafar was gone, all of his magic spells were reversing. Rajah, Abu, and the Magic Carpet returned to their original forms. The Sultan's royal clothes and crown were back, too.

Jasmine sighed with relief. She watched as the Genie picked up Jafar's lamp. "Ten thousand years in the Cave of Wonders ought to chill him out," he announced. He flung the lamp toward the horizon, farther than the human eye could see.

At that, Jasmine laughed out loud. The nightmare was over!

ALADDIN'S THIRD WISH

On the palace balcony, Jasmine and Aladdin stood gazing at each other. Now that Jafar had been defeated, the palace was getting back to normal. The Sultan had immediately freed Amina, who was none the worse for wear. The servants were busy fixing all the damage Jafar had done. Now, Jasmine and Aladdin had found a quiet moment together, and the time had come to put all the lies behind them.

"Jasmine, I'm sorry I lied to you about being a prince," Aladdin said.

"I know why you did." Jasmine smiled at him. She knew that it hadn't been ambition or greed that had made him do it—he had done it out of love. That didn't make it right, but it made it easier to forgive.

"Well, I guess this is good-bye," Aladdin said sadly.

Jasmine couldn't answer for a moment. It just didn't seem fair—they loved each other. But the law said she had to marry a prince, and Aladdin wasn't a prince. She glanced at her father, who was standing nearby. He looked sad, too.

The Genie was looking on. "Al, no problem," he said. "You've still got one wish left. Just say the word and you're a prince again!"

"But Genie, what about your freedom?" Aladdin protested. He had promised to use his third and final wish to free the Genie from his life of servitude. After all the Genie had done for him, he didn't want to go back on his word.

"This is love," the Genie replied. "Al, you're not

going to find another girl like her in a million years!"

Aladdin turned and looked into Jasmine's eyes. The Genie was right—he would never, ever meet anyone else like her. "Jasmine, I do love you," he said, his heart heavy. "But I've got to stop pretending to be something I'm not."

"I understand," Jasmine whispered, feeling as though her heart would break. Part of her wished that Aladdin would change his mind. But she also knew he wouldn't be the person she loved if he turned his back on the Genie.

Aladdin took a deep breath.

"Genie, I wish for your freedom! You're free."

A powerful whirlwind swirled around the

surprised Genie. His iron cuffs broke open, and the lamp fell to the ground, its magic gone.

The Genie laughed in amazement. "I'm free!" he cried.

Jasmine smiled as she watched him holler with joy. She knew how precious freedom was. Even if she was still trapped in her golden cage, she was glad the Genie could enjoy his freedom.

The Genie swooped down to wrap Aladdin in a grateful hug. "No matter what anybody says, you'll always be a prince to me."

"That's right!" the Sultan spoke up suddenly. "You've certainly proved your worth as far as I'm concerned." He shook his head. "It's that law that's the real problem." Then his face broke into a smile. "Well, am I Sultan, or am I Sultan?" he exclaimed.

"From this day forth, the princess can marry whom-ever she deems worthy!"

Jasmine hardly dared to believe her ears. Had her father really done it? Maybe he *did* understand her—much better than she had ever imagined!

"Him!" she burst out joyfully, leaping into Aladdin's waiting arms. "I choose—I choose you, Aladdin!"

Aladdin smiled, holding her tight. "Call me Al," he said.

Jasmine closed her eyes as their lips met in a loving and meaningful kiss. And this time, she knew that nothing would stop them from living happily ever after.

THE STORY OF
ESMERALDA

THE LIFE OF A GYPSY

They say that Paris is the most modern of cities, full of modern people with modern ideas, where one can grow accustomed to seeing travelers from faraway places from all over the world. But no one is ever happy to see me. That's because I am a gypsy.

The life of a gypsy is difficult and dangerous. Most people believe that all gypsies are thieves. When they see us, mothers pull their children close for fear that we will spirit them away. People like to have us tell their future by reading their palms, but if they don't like what we tell them, they say that we're all witches, anyway. Nobody seems to understand that gypsies are just people. Just as is true of everyone else, there are good and bad among us.

The soldiers especially don't believe there can be any good in a gypsy. They think we are all bad, and cause us trouble whenever they can.

One night, as I was dancing on the street with my little goat, Djali, trying to earn a few coins for food, a pair of guards appeared.

"All right, gypsy," one of the men said with a sneer as he eyed my sack of coins. "Where did you get the money?"

"For your information, I earned it!" I told them.

"Gypsies don't earn money," the guard said.

His companion nodded. "They steal it," he added.

Now I was truly angry. How many times have I seen the soldiers rob gypsies of their money before tossing them out of the city or throwing them in prison? "You would know a lot about stealing!" I cried.

"Troublemaker, huh?" the first guard said with a growl, grabbing for my bag.

I wasn't going to let my money go without a fight. Those coins were the only way Djali and I would eat that day. I yanked the bag back. Djali did his part, butting and kicking the men. We managed to pull away and run.

"Come back here, gypsy!" yelled one of the guards.

Glancing back, I saw them running after us. Djali and I are quick, but the guards were big and strong, and the streets were crowded. For a moment, I was sure they would catch us.

Then, a white horse stepped between us and them. The guards crashed right into it. To my surprise, the horse sat down—right on the two men!

The horse's rider was tall, with a blond beard and handsome face. I'd noticed him watching me dance earlier.

"Oh, dear, I'm sorry," the man told the guards,

though he didn't sound sorry at all. "Naughty horse. Naughty."

One of the guards drew his sword. "I'll teach you a lesson, peasant!" he shouted.

At that moment, the man with the horse flipped back his cape. Beneath it, he wore the uniform of a captain of the army. He drew his own sword.

"You were saying, lieutenant?" he said to the guard pleasantly.

The guards fell all over themselves, apologizing to the captain, but I didn't stick around to hear it. It was time for Djali and me to disappear while we still had the chance.

We ran into an alley. Moments later, we were disguised as an old beggar, a cape covering the two of us. A hat sat before us on the street for people's offerings.

Before long, we heard the same two guards coming our way. This time they were shouting for people to move aside.

"You!" one of them shouted at a passerby. "Make way for the captain!"

"Make way!" the other echoed.

I peered out from under the cloak and saw a blond, bearded man striding along. He paused right in front of us. I gulped. Was he looking at us? Did he know we were in here?

If so, he didn't say a word. He merely dropped a few coins in our hat and moved on.

Whew! I was relieved. As soon as the men were out of sight, Djali and I ran in the other direction. However, I couldn't stop thinking about that captain. Had he helped me on purpose? I didn't know, but I soon decided it didn't really matter one way or the other. A smart gypsy never trusts a soldier.

When we were far enough away, I stopped to count our money. There wasn't nearly enough for a

meal, so Djali and I found another good spot and began to dance again.

Soon, a small crowd had gathered to watch us. I smiled as the little goat leaped about near me. Djali loves to dance just as much as I do. Looking at him now, one would never guess at his sad start in life.

When I was just a little girl, my cousin Marco showed me an orchard he'd found. He wanted us to go in and pick fruit to eat.

"That's stealing," I told him.

He shook his head. "Look, cousin," he said. "There are so many pears on those trees that they're falling to the ground and rotting." He smiled at me. "We'll only take the ones that have already fallen. What's the harm in that?"

I hesitated. The plan still made me nervous. But I was hungry, and the sweet smell of ripe pears drifted toward me on the breeze.

Finally, I nodded. "All right," I agreed. "But we can only take the ones that have fallen."

We hurried in among the trees, watching nervously for the farmer. I started gathering the fallen pears, cradling them in my skirt.

Then I noticed Marco climbing one of the trees. "Hey, what are you doing?" I called to him.

"Don't worry," he said as he plucked a perfect, ripe pear from a branch. "This one was about to fall."

Before I could answer, there was an angry shout. Glancing over my shoulder, I saw a man rushing toward us, dragging a sad-looking young goat behind him on a rope.

"Look out!" I shouted.

Marco swung down from the tree. "Run!" he cried.

I started to do as he said, but my foot got caught on a tree root. I fell, spilling all the pears I had gathered. Seconds later, the farmer was towering over me.

"Gypsies!" he shouted. "I should have known!" He grabbed me by the arm and pulled me to my feet. Then he turned to scowl at the little goat. "They steal almost as much of my best fruit as you, worthless beast. I should toss the two of you into the river!"

"Please, sir!" I cried, trying to pull away. Marco had disappeared, leaving me alone. "We didn't mean any harm."

"No harm?" the farmer yelled. "You call stealing my property no harm? I'll show you harm, you little thief!"

He pulled back his hand as if to strike me. But before he could do so, he let out a yelp and leaped forward, dropping my arm and grabbing his own backside. Surprised, I saw the little goat standing there. He had just butted the nasty farmer!

"Run!" I called to the goat, suddenly hopeful again.

This time I didn't trip. I ran as fast as I could, jumping over the stone wall at the edge of the orchard. The little goat leaped right beside me, then stopped short with a bleat.

"What's wrong?" I asked, spinning around.

I saw that the rope around the goat's neck had gotten caught between two of the stones. The frightened animal yanked and twisted, trying with all his might to get free, but the rope was stuck fast.

All of a sudden, there was a shout. It was the farmer. He was coming after us—fast!

I gulped. If I ran now, I would escape the farmer's wrath, for sure. But that would mean leaving behind the goat that had helped me.

No, I couldn't do it. Instead, I raced back toward the stone wall. It only took a few seconds to free the goat from the rope, but that was almost enough time for the farmer to catch up to us.

"You go that way," I said to the goat, pointing to the left. "I'll go this way. He can't chase us both!"

The goat seemed to understand. We ran off in opposite directions, leaving the farmer cursing behind us. Once we were sure we'd lost him, we found each other again by the river. And brave little Djali has been my constant companion ever since.

THE FESTIVAL OF FOOLS

I made more money than usual dancing that day. The people of Paris were in a good and generous mood. That was probably because it was a festival day—soon the Festival of Fools would begin. It was a day for laughter, pranks, celebration, and fun. A day when all of Paris seemed to turn upside down and inside out.

Along with everyone else in Paris, I hurried to the main square in front of Notre Dame cathedral to join in the fun. Clopin, the leader of the gypsies, was already there when I arrived, leading the crowd in song and dance. Everyone was dressed up, and many wore masks. Some of these masks were beautiful, others were funny, while still others were hideous or frightening.

Some people tottered along on stilts, while others dragged small children by the hand. On a tightrope strung high above the square, a gypsy I knew thrilled everyone with his daring tricks. Musicians played cheerful music on the huge stage set up for the occasion, while many members of the audience danced and sang along. Altogether, it was a wonderful, busy, noisy, crowded, exciting scene.

Soon it would be my turn to dance, so I hurried into a gypsy tent to change my clothes. As I pulled on a robe, I heard a commotion behind me.

"Hey!" I cried, startled.

When I turned around, I saw that someone had stumbled into my tent and tripped over a stool. Djali was staring at him suspiciously, but I wasn't really nervous. I always had my dagger with me in case of emergencies. My cousin, Marco, gave it to me long ago—just after that trip to the orchard, in fact.

The stranger was wearing a hood, so it was hard to see his face. But it looked as though he was also wearing a mask. I suspected he was just a festivalgoer who had enjoyed a little too much wine.

"Are you all right?" I asked, bending over him.

"I—I didn't mean to," he said with a gasp, pulling his hood still lower. "I'm sorry."

His voice was soft and sounded kind. "Well, you're not hurt, are you?" I asked him. "Here, let's see."

I made a move to pull back his hood. He tried to edge away, but I was too quick for him. Soon his mask was revealed—a scary and hideous mask. Mismatched eyes bulged above a misshapen nose,

and I saw that a humped back was part of the costume as well. The mask was so lifelike that it was
hard to see where it ended and where the man's
skin began.

A quick look showed that he was fine. "Just try to
be a little more careful," I told him with a chuckle.

"I—I will," he whispered. Then he hurried out
through the tent flap.

"By the way," I called after him—"great mask!"

After that, I had to hurry to get ready. I heard Clopin singing out my introduction. I smiled as he referred to me as "the finest girl in France." Straightening my skirt, I vowed to live up to his words by dancing my best.

I stepped forward as Clopin finished the introduction. "Dance, la Esmeralda, dance!" he cried.

Then he flung down a handful of colorful powder on the stage. There was a puff of red smoke, and when it cleared, Clopin was gone and I was standing in his place.

I smiled as the crowd roared its approval.

Then I began my dance. It was easy to lose myself in the movement, but I had learned long ago to stay alert. That was the only way to avoid being captured by soldiers.

Today, I had little worry about that. But I did

notice that Judge Claude Frollo was sitting in a special viewing stand in the audience. Even though he was a good distance away, I still felt a shudder of fear. Judge Frollo had long ago declared himself the mortal enemy of all gypsies. He was determined to rid Paris of us entirely if he could. It was by his orders that the guards harassed us, and at his hands that my mother, my father, and many other friends and relatives had disappeared.

However, I would never let Frollo know that he scared me. Instead, I danced toward him. As I approached, I saw another familiar face at his side—it was the captain from earlier! I was surprised and disappointed. It seemed that I had been right not to trust the handsome soldier. He was Frollo's new Captain of the Guard, and that meant he was my enemy.

Frollo's somber face grew darker as I approached him, dancing and twirling to the beat of the music. I

leaped across to the viewing
stand and landed right in
front of him. Leaning
toward him, I wrapped my
scarf around his neck to the
howls of the crowd. Frollo

scowled at me and yanked the scarf free as I danced
away.

When I returned to the stage, I noticed the
masked fellow who had stumbled into my tent,
watching at the edge of the crowd. I winked at him,
which made him pull the hood over his face. I
almost laughed out loud. He was a shy one!

I continued dancing. By the time I finished, the
audience was in a frenzy. I could tell that Clopin
was pleased as he leaped past me to introduce the
next bit of entertainment—it was time to crown the
King of Fools!

This was one of the highlights of the celebration.
The crowd always chose the most horrible, gruesome,
frightening face in Paris to be king for the day. That

was why people worked so hard on their masks—
everyone wanted the chance to compete for the crown!

As I listened to Clopin explaining the contest to
the crowd, I spotted my masked friend from before.
Perfect! I thought. His mask was so hideous and so
real that he was sure to win!

I reached down and grabbed my friend by the
hand, pulling him up onstage. A number of other
people in masks had already gathered on the stage,
and I pushed him out among them.

Then, as Clopin sang to the crowd, urging them
to vote with their voices, I began pulling off the
contestants' masks.

First, I pulled off the mask of a man wearing a
horse costume. He grunted and made an ugly face.
But it wasn't enough for the crowd. They booed and
jeered, and Djali butted the man off the stage.

I moved on to the next contestant, and the next,
but the result was always the same. None of the
faces was ugly enough for the audience.

Finally, I came to my friend from the tent. I

reached up, preparing to grab his mask. But instead of soft fabric or hide, my fingers felt only human skin. I stepped back in shock.

"That's no mask!" a man in the crowd shouted.

"It's his face!" a woman's voice added, sounding as shocked as I felt.

There were more murmurs and shouts. "He's hideous!" someone cried.

"It's the bell ringer from Notre Dame!" someone else called out.

Meanwhile, the man clapped his hands over his face. "Oh," he moaned. "Oh, oh!"

He was terrified and humiliated. While I still felt horrified at his appearance, I also felt guilty. It was my fault he was up here—I had exposed him to the ridicule of the crowd.

Meanwhile, Clopin took advantage of the uproar. "Ladies and gentlemen, don't panic," he cried. "We asked for the ugliest face in Paris, and here he is! Quasimodo, the Hunchback of Notre Dame!"

With that, the cries of horror turned to laughter. Several people leaped up onto the stage and lifted Quasimodo to their shoulders. They carried him to a litter and then hoisted him into the air.

Now I knew who the unfortunate man with the twisted face was. I had heard tales of the bell ringer who lived high atop the Cathedral of Notre Dame, ringing the bells at the appointed times, never coming out into the city. People said he was a ward of Judge Frollo, that the judge had saved the infant Quasimodo from gypsies.

I watched as the litter was carried all around the square, the crowd singing and shouting the new King of Fools' praises. At first Quasimodo looked nervous, but soon he relaxed. After a few minutes, he even seemed to be enjoying himself. He smiled and waved as the enormous crowd cheered him on.

I felt relieved as I wandered toward the tent. Perhaps I hadn't done him a bad turn, after all.

A few minutes later, as I glanced out of the tent, I saw that Quasimodo was being returned to the stage. I smiled as an old lady tossed him a bouquet of flowers. Others were throwing colorful confetti, which rained down around him. Quasimodo was smiling, seeming overwhelmed but pleased by the attention.

Then, an overripe tomato flew threw the air, landing on Quasimodo's face. "Long live the king!" someone jeered from the crowd.

I gasped in horror. More fruits and vegetables were already raining down on Quasimodo as others caught on to the cruel joke. Quasimodo tried to escape, but his foot slipped on a slimy bit of tomato. He fell to his knees as the crowd shouted with laughter. A couple of men slipped ropes around him, trapping him in place.

"Where are you going, hunchback?" someone shouted.

Quasimodo had nowhere to turn and no way to escape. I saw him glance at Judge Frollo, who was watching the whole scene from the viewing platform. The captain looked concerned, but Frollo's face was impassive. He made no move to help as the crowd continued jeering and pelting Quasimodo with anything the people could find—not only fruits and vegetables but stones as well.

I couldn't take it anymore. I leaped back onto the stage. "I'm sorry," I whispered to the miserable Quasimodo. "This wasn't supposed to happen." I wiped his face with my scarf.

Then, I turned to face the crowd. They had stopped throwing things when I got in the way. But they were still howling with awful, uncontrollable mirth. Meanwhile, Frollo was scowling at me.

"You!" he said. "Gypsy girl. Get down at once!"

I kneeled beside Quasimodo. "Yes, Your Honor," I told the judge. "Just as soon as I free this poor creature."

"I forbid it!" Frollo shouted furiously.

I had no idea why the judge would wish this humiliation on one who was supposed to be his ward. But I didn't care what his reasons were. Surely, they were no better than the reasons why he sent his soldiers after the gypsies. It only took a second to cut the ropes with my dagger.

"How dare you defy me?" Frollo hissed.

I stood and faced him. "You mistreat this poor boy the same way you mistreat my people!" I cried. "You speak of justice, yet you are cruel to those most in need of your help!"

"Silence!" Frollo roared.

I refused to heed him. "Justice!" I shouted in return, raising my fist in the air.

Frollo's face was pinched with rage. "Mark my words, gypsy," he told me. "You will pay for this insolence!"

"Then, it appears we've crowned the wrong fool," I taunted him. "The only fool I see is you!" I flung Quasimodo's "crown" at the judge and then leaped offstage into the crowd.

I was lucky the square was so crowded. Even though I could hear Frollo ordering his men to seize and arrest me, I knew I would be able to escape—this time, at least.

But I also knew I'd better stay out of Frollo's sight from now on. After seeing how he had treated his ward, Quasimodo, I didn't want to imagine what he would do if he ever caught me.

FRIEND OR FOE?

It was cool and dark inside the cathedral, where I stopped for refuge a short while later. I knew I would be safe there for the moment. Even Frollo wouldn't dare seize anyone inside the church. Such actions were strictly forbidden—the cathedral was a place of shelter for those in need.

Breathing in the scents of burning candles and incense, I wondered just what had happened. It surely had not been wise to provoke the most powerful, most feared man in Paris. But what else could I have done? I couldn't stand by and watch as he allowed poor Quasimodo to be mistreated.

As I thought about that, wondering why the bell ringer had emerged from his tower after all this time, I suddenly became aware of someone creeping up behind me. Acting on instinct, I whirled around. A second later, my pursuer was on the ground, with my hand holding his own sword at his throat.

To my amazement, it was the Captain of the Guard. "You!" I cried, realizing that my escape must not have been quite as clever as I had thought. Perhaps the soldier had recognized my beggar's out-fit, which I had used to slip away from the crowd and enter here.

"Easy, easy!" the man said nervously. "Uh, I—I just shaved this morning."

I almost smiled at his quip. But I didn't pull back the sword. "Oh, really?" I retorted. "You missed a spot."

"All right, all right," the man said. "Just calm down. Give me a chance to apologize."

I was surprised. "For what?" I asked.

Instead of replying, the soldier suddenly grabbed the sword out of my hands. With a quick toss, he sent me tumbling to the floor.

"That, for example," he said.

I was furious—and nervous. Fortunately, he didn't seem anxious to use the sword against me. "Are you always this charming?" I snapped. "Or am I just lucky?"

As I spoke, I grabbed a candelabrum and swung it at him. He blocked the blow easily with his sword. Obviously, he was much quicker than most.

Still, I wasn't about to give up. I was sure Frollo had sent him for me. I continued swinging the candelabrum at him. Soon, he was panting with the effort of avoiding my blows.

"You fight almost as well as a man," he said.

"Funny," I replied. "I was going to say the same thing about you!"

Finally, I landed a blow with the candelabrum, striking him on the jaw. Djali had been hiding since the man's appearance, but now he leaped forward to help, butting the soldier in the stomach.

The man grunted. "Didn't know you had a kid," he joked weakly. I was about to strike him again, but something stopped me. For a soldier, this man didn't seem to be trying very hard to hurt me. "Uh, permit me," he said as I stared down at him. "I'm Phoebus. It means 'sun god.'"

I blinked. It was a very strange name for a soldier—or for anyone.

"And you are?" Phoebus prompted.

Suddenly suspicious again, I glared at him. "Is this an interrogation?"

He put away his sword. "It's called an introduction," he replied with a smile.

"You're not arresting me?" I asked.

"Not as long as you're in here," he said. "I can't."

I was a bit surprised. When I'd seen him behind me, I had been sure he was going to defy the sanctuary of the church and grab me. It wouldn't be unlike Frollo's men to do just that.

"Huh?" I said. "You're not at all like the other soldiers."

"Thank you." Phoebus smiled.

When he asked my name again, I decided there was no harm in answering. "Esmeralda," I said.

"Beautiful," he responded. "Much better than Phoebus, anyway."

At that moment, a new voice interrupted. "Good work, captain. Now arrest her."

I gasped. It was Frollo! He was standing with a small group of soldiers, blocking the doorway. Djali cowered behind me as I stared at them in horror.

"Claim sanctuary!" Phoebus whispered behind me. "Say it!"

"You tricked me!" I said accusingly. What was I thinking? He worked for Frollo—our greatest enemy!

Phoebus turned to address Frollo. "I'm sorry, sir," he said. "She claimed sanctuary. There's nothing I can do."

Frollo scowled. "Then drag her outside and—"

"Frollo!" another voice broke in. "You will not touch her."

This time it was the Archdeacon, the head of the cathedral. He glared at Frollo, then glanced toward me. "Don't worry," he said. "Minister Frollo learned years ago to respect the sanctity of the church."

The Archdeacon ordered the soldiers out, and I thought I was safe. But as Frollo turned to leave, he grabbed me by the arm.

"You think you've outwitted me," he said, hissing in my ear. "But I am a patient man. And gypsies

don't do well inside stone walls. You've chosen a
magnificent prison, but it is a prison, nonetheless."
He sneered as he released me and walked toward
the door. "Set one foot outside, and you're mine!"

MEETING A MONSTER

I slumped to the floor. It was true—I was trapped! There was only a handful of exits leading out of the cathedral. Frollo could easily order his soldiers to guard all of them. There was no escape!

Still, I couldn't just give up. "If Frollo thinks he can keep us here, he's wrong!" I said fiercely.

The Archdeacon glanced at me. "Don't act rashly, my child," he said quietly. "You created quite a stir at the festival. It would be unwise to arouse Frollo's anger further."

"You saw what he did out there," I reminded the priest. "Letting the crowd torture that poor boy!"

The Archdeacon shook his head sadly. "You can't right all the wrongs of this world by yourself."

That was true enough, I realized. But did that mean I shouldn't even try? That didn't seem right. Quasimodo had been all alone up there, an outcast from society, just because he looked different from most people. I knew exactly how that felt—I was an outcast, too, only because I was a gypsy.

As I stared at the statues and stained-glass windows in the cathedral, wondering what to do, I 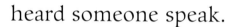 heard someone speak.

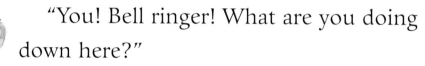 "You! Bell ringer! What are you doing down here?"

I turned and saw a churchgoer glaring angrily toward the stairs. When I followed his gaze, I saw Quasimodo cowering there.

"Haven't you caused enough trouble already?" the churchgoer asked angrily.

Quasimodo turned and started to hurry away.

But I stepped forward. "Wait," I called to him. "I want to talk to you."

Before the sentence was out of my mouth, Quasimodo had disappeared up the stairs. I followed, running up the staircase with Djali at my heels.

I caught up to him on a high parapet wall. Several stone gargoyles guarded the place, which offered a beautiful view of the city below.

"Here you are!" I exclaimed, panting a bit from the chase. "I was afraid I'd lost you."

Quasimodo looked nervous. "Yes," he said. "Uh, I have chores to do. I-i-it was nice seeing you again."

"Wait!" I cried again. I wasn't going to let him get away without his hearing what I wanted to say. "I'm really sorry about this afternoon. I had no idea who you were. I would never have pulled you up on the stage."

He was still trying to escape, climbing up a ladder leading to yet another level. I followed him again and emerged into a sort of apartment high above the cathedral. It held a few bits of furniture, including a table with a tiny model version of the city of Paris. The great iron bells of Notre Dame were visible nearby.

I stared around curiously. "What is this place?"

"This is where I live," Quasimodo answered shyly.

I stepped forward for a better look at the table. "Did you make all these things yourself?" I was amazed at the detail in the models—tiny buildings, tiny animals, tiny everything! "This is beautiful! If I could do this, you wouldn't find me dancing in the street for coins!"

"But you're a wonderful dancer!" Quasimodo protested.

"Well, it keeps bread on the table." I noticed that part of the city model was covered by a cloth. I reached for it, wondering what was underneath: "What's this?"

"Oh, no, please!" Quasimodo cried. "I—I'm not finished. I still have to paint them."

But I had already seen the little human figures underneath. I even recognized some of them. "It's the blacksmith!" I cried with delight. "And the baker! You're a surprising person, Quasimodo. Not to mention, lucky. All this room to yourself?" I could hardly imagine it. I had never even had a corner of a room all to myself in my life!

Quasimodo shrugged. "Well, it's not just me. There's the gargoyles, and of course the bells. Would you like to see them?" he asked.

"Yes, of course!" I could tell the bells were special to him. "Wouldn't we, Djali?" I added warningly to the goat, who was about to chew on one of the tiny figurines.

Quasimodo took us on a tour of the many bells of Notre Dame. He had names for each of them—Little Sophia, Jeanne-Marie, Big Marie, and many more. After that, he showed us the view over Paris from the bell tower. It was breathtaking—the city looked beautiful and peaceful from high up there.

"I could stay up here forever!" I exclaimed.

"Y-you could, you know," Quasimodo suggested.

I shook my head. "No, I couldn't. Gypsies don't do well inside stone walls."

"But you're not like the other gypsies. They are—evil!" he exclaimed.

I frowned, surprised that such a belief would come out of such a gentle soul. "Who told you that?" I demanded.

"My master, Frollo," Quasimodo said. "He raised me. He took me in when no one else would. I am a monster, you know."

"He told you that?" I asked. I should have guessed. Only an evil man like Frollo could fill Quasimodo's mind with such nasty ideas.

Quasimodo seemed sad. "Just look at me," he murmured.

Knowing that I had caused him still more pain earlier at the festival, I wanted to help him feel a little better if I could. "Give me your hand," I said.

Then I pretended to read his palm. I pointed out his long lifeline and another line indicating his shyness. Then I stared more closely.

"Hmm, that's funny," I said. "I don't see any monster lines. Not a single one." I held out my own hand toward him. "Now you look at me. Do you think *I'm* evil?"

"No!" he cried immediately. "You are kind and good and . . . and . . ."

"And a gypsy," I finished for him. "And maybe Frollo's wrong about both of us."

He seemed willing to think about that. In the

meantime, my mind was returning to my own problems. How was I going to escape? There just didn't seem to be a way.

Quasimodo guessed what I was thinking. "You helped me," he said. "Now I will help you."

"But there's no way out," I said sadly. "There are soldiers at every door."

"We won't use a door," Quasimodo said.

"You mean, climb down?" I asked in amazement, glancing over the wall at the ground far, far below.

"Sure," Quasimodo said. He gestured toward Djali. "You carry him," he told me, "and I carry you."

It hardly seemed possible. But I was willing to try anything to escape the prison Frollo had made of the cathedral. "Come on, Djali," I said.

The little goat jumped into my arms, and then Quasimodo lifted us up. His arms were surprisingly strong.

"Don't be afraid," he told me.

"I am not afraid," I replied, though that wasn't entirely true.

Quasimodo grabbed a gargoyle for support, then swung over the wall. We were up so high that the ground seemed farther away than ever! But the bell ringer didn't hesitate. He swung around the side of the tower, confident and sure.

Soon we were making our way down the outside walls of the cathedral. I hardly dared to watch. At one point, a bit of the roof broke off, and we slid

partway down. But Quasimodo managed to grab a part of a buttress before the roof piece flew off into space. Moments later, we were safely on the ground, out of sight of the guards.

"I hope I didn't scare you," Quasimodo whispered.

"Not for an instant." I lied gratefully. Suddenly, I had a wonderful idea. "Come with me," I told him.

"What?" he asked in disbelief.

"To the Court of Miracles," I explained. That was the name of the gypsy hideaway deep beneath the city. Everyone knew of its existence, though we gypsies were the only ones who knew how to get there. "Leave this place."

"Oh, no." Quasimodo shook his head. "I'm never going back out there again. You saw what happened today. This is where I belong."

"All right," I said, seeing that his mind was made up. "Then I'll come to see you." Still, I felt I owed the bell ringer some token of my thanks. He had risked everything for me.

Then I had another idea. I reached up and

removed the necklace I was wearing, with its elaborate woven amulet. I handed it to him.

"If *you* ever need sanctuary," I told him, "this will
show you the way." Then I quoted the rhyme I'd
been taught as a child. "When you wear this woven
band, you hold the city in your hand."

Djali was getting restless, and I knew it was time

to leave before the guards heard us. While Quasimodo tucked the amulet beneath his shirt, the little goat and I dashed off into the darkness.

As I rounded a corner heading away from the cathedral, I heard a soft whistle. I recognized my cousin's signal. "Marco!" I cried, spying him in a doorway.

"How did you manage to get out of the cathedral?" he asked me in amazement.

"It would take too long to explain," I answered, glancing around nervously at the sound of the guards doing their rounds nearby. We stayed still and silent until we were sure they had passed.

"I know a safe place where you can spend the night," Marco said. "Not our people, but they're good, and we can trust them."

I nodded without another word.

My cousin took me to the home of a miller just outside the city. One of the servants led us to the barn, where we could spend the night.

I settled into the pile of straw with relief. It had been a very long day. With my head resting on Djali's soft belly, I fell asleep almost immediately.

FLAMES OF ANGER

The next morning, we slipped away early. Marco went in one direction, and Djali and I in another. We had only walked a short distance from the mill when I heard shouts from somewhere behind us.

"What was that?" I murmured. The nervous feeling in my stomach told me it could not be good news.

I sneaked back through the fields for a look. To my horror, I saw soldiers wandering around in the yard outside the mill where I'd stayed the night before. Were they there looking for me? How had they known?

Pulling the beggar disguise over myself and the goat, I watched from a distance. When no one seemed to notice me, I moved a little closer, weaving in among the crowd of onlookers, wanting to hear what was going on.

"Poor miller," a woman said, shaking her head as she watched the soldiers stomp in and out of the mill. "He's never harmed anyone."

A man nodded his agreement. "Frollo's gone mad," he commented.

Just then, I spotted Frollo himself. He was questioning the miller. "Have you been harboring gypsies?" he demanded.

"Our home is always open to the weary traveler," the miller responded. "Have mercy, my lord. I assure you, we know nothing of these gypsies."

Frollo's soldiers exited the mill. I saw that Phoebus was among them. Then Frollo himself shut the door and slid a spear through the door latch, locking the miller and his family inside.

The judge looked at Phoebus, who was holding a torch. "Burn it," he ordered.

I gasped in shock. Phoebus looked startled. "What?" he exclaimed.

"Until it smolders," Frollo added.

"With all due respect, sir, I was not trained to murder the innocent," Phoebus said.

Frollo glared at him. "But you *were* trained to follow orders."

Phoebus stared back, and for a moment I feared he would do as Frollo had commanded. For some reason, this seemed more terrible than anything else that was happening.

But then, the captain took his torch and

dropped it into a bucket of water. The flame was extinguished with a sizzle of steam.

"Insolent coward!" Frollo shouted in anger. And with that, he grabbed a torch from another soldier and lit the mill house ablaze himself!

I was certain that the miller and his family were doomed. And it was all because of me!

But all of a sudden, Phoebus leaped forward. He broke a window and rescued the family. I gasped in amazement. Maybe he really *was* different from the other soldiers!

Then I gasped again, this time in horror. One of Frollo's other soldiers had just sneaked up and

knocked Phoebus down with his sword! Frollo himself was riding toward him on his horse.

"The sentence for insubordination," Frollo announced coldly, staring down at Phoebus, "is death. Such a pity. You threw away a promising career."

Phoebus glared at Frollo, but I didn't wait to see what he would do. Grabbing a stone, I ran forward and flung it at Frollo's horse, using my scarf as a slingshot.

My aim was good. The stone struck the horse on its hindquarters, startling it. It reared and bucked, throwing Frollo to the ground.

Phoebus sprang to his feet. Pushing away the confused soldiers, he leaped onto Frollo's horse.

"Get him!" Frollo screamed as Phoebus rode off. "And don't hit my horse!"

The other men raced after Phoebus. Arrows flew through the air all around him. Phoebus galloped across a bridge, heading for the woods. But just when I hoped that he might be able to escape,

an arrow struck him in the back. He tumbled off the horse and over the edge of the bridge into the river.

I ran toward the water, with Djali following close behind.

Frollo didn't see me—he was looking down into the river. "Don't waste your arrows," he told his men as they prepared to shoot again. "Let the traitor rot in his watery grave.

"Now find the girl!" he added. "If you have to burn the city to the ground, so be it!"

He was talking about me. I should have run for the woods myself, but I couldn't leave Phoebus behind. Especially after he had been so noble and brave. I had to see if he was still alive.

As soon as the soldiers were gone, I dove into the river. Phoebus was floating facedown, and for a moment I almost gave up hope.

But I had to try to rescue him. I swam toward him, and as soon as I touched him, I realized he

was still alive. The wound from the arrow was bleeding a little, but it didn't look too bad up close.

Hooking my arm under his, I held him tightly and swam for the shore.

THE COURT OF MIRACLES

"Quasimodo?" I called, panting as I reached the top of the staircase leading to the bell tower. I had never been so tired in all my life. It had taken everything I had to get Phoebus this far. Luckily, a friend, a gypsy named Homer, had found me struggling to carry the soldier. After hearing the tale, he had offered to help me sneak the injured man back into the cathedral. I think he liked the idea of putting one over on the evil Frollo.

"Esmeralda?" Quasimodo's soft voice replied to my call. He sounded surprised.

It was no wonder he sounded that way. Half of Paris was on fire—I could hardly believe that Frollo was willing to destroy so much just to find me!

"You're all right!" Quasimodo cried, hugging me. "I knew you'd come back."

I was glad to see him. But this was no time for pleasantries. "You've done so much for me already, my friend. But I must ask for your help one more time," I begged.

"Yes," he said immediately. "Anything."

I was relieved. At my signal, Homer carried Phoebus into the room.

"This is Phoebus," I told Quasimodo. "He's wounded and a fugitive like me. He can't go on much longer. I knew he'd be safe here. Please, can you hide him?"

Quasimodo gestured for Homer to follow. "This way."

Soon Phoebus was resting in Quasimodo's own bed. The wounded soldier had been unconscious for most of the journey, but now he opened his eyes and looked up at me.

"Esmeralda," he said weakly.

I shushed him. "You'll hide here until you're strong enough to move."

Quasimodo brought a bottle of wine, which I used to clean Phoebus's wound. I could tell it was very painful, but he gritted his teeth and told jokes while I did my doctoring.

As I was stitching the wound, Phoebus let out a

groan. "Why is it, whenever we meet, I end up bleeding?" he quipped.

"You're lucky," I said as I bit the thread to cut it. "That arrow almost pierced your heart."

He caught my hand, holding it against his chest. "I'm not so sure it didn't," he replied.

I stared down at him. He gazed back at me. For a moment, I found myself lost in his eyes. He pulled me closer, and our lips met in a sweet kiss.

The tender moment was interrupted when I heard Djali bleat with fright out on the balcony. A moment later, Quasimodo called to me, sounding frantic.

"Frollo's coming!" he cried. "You must leave!"

He led me to a different staircase. Homer had already disappeared. I paused before running down, touching Quasimodo's hand.

"Be careful, my friend," I told him. "Promise you won't let anything happen to him."

"I promise," Quasimodo replied.

Soon Djali and I were slipping through the streets of Paris. The air was full of smoke, and a reddish glare lit up the night. It was horrible. There was only one place I could go to feel safe.

A little while later, I was pushing back the lid of a tomb in the cemetery. Stairs led down through the tomb into the old catacombs beneath the city. That was the place the gypsies called the Court of Miracles, the one safe hideaway Frollo had never been able to discover and destroy.

When I reached the main living area, Clopin was waiting there for me. "Welcome back, la Esmeralda," he said without smiling. "I suppose you know you are the reason for this fireworks display. Frollo is burning down half of Paris, and every gypsy that he sees is a dead man."

"I am not the reason," I said, correcting him.

 "Frollo himself is the one who has gone crazy." I shrugged. "He has always hated us. I am only today's convenient excuse." I sat down at the table and cut myself a piece of bread.

Clopin sighed. "I suppose you're right. But what do reasons matter? We are all in danger. As long as Frollo lives, we gypsies can have only half a life." He took the bread knife and angrily stabbed it into the wooden table.

As he left the room, I pulled the knife free. Despite what I had told Clopin, I did feel guilty for having set off Frollo's rage. But what else could I have done? Let Quasimodo be tormented for the amusement of the crowd?

No, I had only done what I had to do. And I knew at least one other person could understand how I felt—Phoebus, too, had risked everything to do what he thought was right. Knowing that made me care for him all the more. I hoped he was all right. I knew Quasimodo would take good care of him. Phoebus's wound was not life-threatening. All he needed was to rest quietly.

And so did I. "Come on, Djali," I told the goat. "Let's go find someplace to lie down for a while."

I don't know how long I slept. It was Djali who awoke me. He bleated urgently.

"What is it?" I asked, my voice weary and a little annoyed. "What's the matter now?"

Djali danced on his little hooves, seeming more frantic than ever. Finally, I awoke and realized that something must be really wrong.

"Okay, I'm coming," I said, jumping to my feet. "Lead the way."

When we burst into a cavern in the catacombs, the first thing I saw was a large crowd of gypsies gathered together around the stage where an old gallows sat. There were two men standing beneath the strong wooden beam tied with nooses. I rubbed my eyes, trying to figure out what was going on.

Suddenly, I recognized the two men in the nooses.

"Stop!" I screamed, hustling through the crowd.

Clopin was standing beside the two men. He turned to stare in surprise as Djali and I pushed our way toward him. I knew what had  happened—Quasimodo and Phoebus had followed the map on the necklace I'd given Quasimodo and had come here looking for me. The other gypsies had spotted them and thought they were both working for Frollo.

"These men aren't spies!" I cried as I reached the stage. "They're our friends."

Murmurs rose up in the crowd behind me. Clopin shrugged. "Why didn't they say so?" he asked.

I leaped up onto the stage and quickly untied Phoebus and Quasimodo, removing the gags from their mouths.

"We did say so!" they both cried when they could speak.

I quickly explained that Phoebus was the one who had saved the miller's family, while Quasimodo had helped me escape from Notre Dame. Finally, the other gypsies seemed ready to believe me.

Phoebus stepped forward. "We came to warn you," he said. "Frollo's coming. He says he knows where you're hiding, and he's attacking at dawn with a thousand men!"

I gasped along with the others. I had no idea when or how the pair had learned this terrible news, but I didn't doubt them for a second. If Phoebus and Quasimodo, my two trusted friends, said Frollo was coming, I believed them.

"Let's waste no time. We must leave immediately!" I cried.

There was a flurry of activity as everyone scattered, gathering up their few belongings and waking the children. Meanwhile, I turned to Phoebus. Despite everything else, I was happy to see him.

"You took a terrible risk coming here," I said. "It may not exactly show, but we're grateful."

Phoebus smiled, then glanced at his companion. "Don't thank me—thank Quasimodo," he said. "Without his help, I would never have found my way here."

"Nor would I," a voice said from behind.

The voice that spoke those last words sent a chill down my spine. It was Frollo! He was standing in the doorway with a troop of soldiers.

The soldiers raced in. Gypsies screamed and ran for their lives. I looked around desperately for an escape, but there was none. We were surrounded!

CAPTURED

"After twenty years of searching," Frollo exclaimed, "the Court of Miracles is mine at last!" He smirked at Quasimodo. "Dear Quasimodo, I always knew you would someday be of use to me," he said sarcastically.

The bell ringer recoiled in horror. "No!"

I couldn't believe my ears. "What are you talking about, Frollo?" I demanded.

"Why, he led me right to you, my dear," Frollo said.

"You're a liar," I retorted. I knew there was no

way Quasimodo would have betrayed me by bringing Frollo to the Court of Miracles.

Frollo must have followed Quasimodo, unbeknownst to the bell ringer. He betrayed his own ward—using him to find us. And now he had us right where he wanted us. All around me, I saw soldiers taking gypsies prisoner.

Then Frollo stepped toward Phoebus, who was trying to break free from the soldier constraining him. "And look what else I've caught in my net.

Captain Phoebus, back from the dead. Another miracle, no doubt."

"There'll be a little bonfire in the square tomorrow," Frollo announced with obvious glee. "And you're all invited to attend. Lock them up!"

With that, the soldiers dragged us off to prison. They even took away poor Djali.

I spent a miserable night locked in a dank cell with a dozen other gypsies. More of my people were in the adjoining cells. Some of the men talked of escape, but most were silent. We all knew it was useless. This time, there truly seemed to be no way out.

At last, as the night wore on and the others fell silent, I dozed a little. Once, I even began to dream. In my dream, I found a key that opened the cell door. With it, I slipped out and rushed to find Phoebus. I discovered him locked inside his own

cell. Oddly, the cell had no door—only a window blocked by strong iron bars.

Neither of us spoke. I tested the bars with my hands, but even as I did so, I knew the bars would not give. Then Phoebus reached between the bars and took my hands in his own. We stood there for a long moment, still silent, just gazing at each other. . . .

Then I woke up. A sliver of dawn's first light illuminated the cell. All around me, I saw my people huddled together, trying to sleep or just waiting for what was to come.

I could hardly believe it had come to this. Frollo had won—he had stolen our freedom, and soon he would steal our lives.

But I was sure of one thing. He might be able to kill me, but he would never have the satisfaction of seeing me beg for mercy. He would never have my soul.

It wasn't long before soldiers appeared at our cell. They dragged me out alone, leaving the others behind. Leading me outside to the cathedral square, they tied me to a stake. Straw was piled around my feet. Glancing around, I saw that Phoebus along with some of the other gypsies had been brought out and imprisoned in cages nearby.

I also saw that a crowd was gathering. News of the execution must have spread through the city even faster than the flames Frollo's men had started the night before. I was terrified, but I did my best not to let it show.

After a moment, Frollo stepped forward to address the crowd. "The prisoner, Esmeralda, has been found guilty of the crime of witchcraft," he announced. "The sentence—death!"

I heard a few cheers from the crowd, but also a few shouts for my release. But it did no good. The executioner stepped forward, holding a torch. He stared up at me for a moment. Out of the corner of my eye, I saw the Archdeacon step out of the cathedral. But several soldiers blocked his path. He would not be able to save me this time.

Nor would Phoebus. I could see him in his cage, struggling against the iron bars. But just as in my dream, they would not budge.

Frollo stepped forward. He took the torch from

the executioner's hand. I guessed that he wanted to do the deed himself.

"The time has come, gypsy," he said to me. "You stand upon the brink of the abyss." He took a step closer and lowered his voice. "Yet even now it is not too late."

I stared at him. What did he mean by that?

"I can save you from the flames of this world and the next," he went on quietly, his eyes glittering as much as the flame of his torch. "Choose me—or the fire."

Suddenly, I realized what he was offering. If I were to become his slave, he would release me.

There was only one response. I spit in his face.

That brought gasps from the crowd. Frollo looked furious as he wiped away the spittle. When he spoke again, his voice was much more harsh.

"This evil witch has put the soul of every citizen in Paris in mortal jeopardy!" he cried. With that, he lowered the torch and set the kindling at my feet ablaze.

There were cries and murmurs from the crowd. I could already feel the heat around my bare feet as more and more of the kindling caught flame.

For a moment, the only sounds I could hear were the crackling of the fire and the pounding of my own heart. The smoke rose up around me, choking me and making it hard to breathe. Suddenly, I heard a cry:

"Noooooooooo!"

Looking up with one last bit of energy, I gasped in surprise. Quasimodo was swinging down toward me on a rope! A moment later, he leaped onto the platform where I was tied. With a quick jerk, he pulled the ropes loose, freeing me.

I was barely conscious by then, and sank against him as he lifted me onto his shoulder. Soldiers were running toward us, but Quasimodo grabbed a burning plank and swung it at them menacingly.

That was the last thing I remembered before I slipped into darkness.

TRUE HEROES

I swam back to consciousness—and almost immediately wished that I hadn't. Breathing was difficult, and every part of my body hurt. My legs ached and my head was pounding.

But I forced myself to open my eyes. I was in the bell tower. Quasimodo was nearby, but he was not looking at me. He was glaring at Frollo, who stood facing him.

Later, I would learn that Quasimodo had carried me to the steps of Notre Dame. Crying out for sanctuary, he had brought me inside.

But that hadn't stopped Frollo. Ordering his soldiers to seize the cathedral, he had smashed his way inside and followed Quasimodo, ignoring the protests of the Archdeacon. He had followed us all the way up to Quasimodo's bell tower. It is possible Frollo didn't realize that, all around him, the people of Paris were rebelling against him, freeing the other prisoners and fighting the soldiers. Or maybe he was too consumed with his own rage to care.

In any case, at the moment my eyes opened, I knew that Frollo was there.

"Quasimodo!" I gasped.

"Esmeralda!" he exclaimed.

As I pushed myself up into a sitting position, Quasimodo turned and hurried toward me. He looked amazed to see me awake.

Frollo seemed much less happy about it. "She lives," he said. Then he drew his sword.

Quasimodo grabbed me, lifting me in his arms as if I weighed no more than a feather. "No!" he shouted at Frollo. Turning, he raced out of the room with me. We burst out onto a balcony.

A moment later, Frollo followed. "Leaving so soon?" he said with a snicker.

Quasimodo climbed down the parapet. I clung to him for dear life. Frollo was still after us—he was trying to reach Quasimodo's hands and wrists with his sword so that the bell ringer would lose his grip and we would fall.

But Quasimodo knew the walls, gargoyles, and parapets better than Frollo could ever imagine. He swung nimbly off the wall onto a nearby section of roof.

Still, Frollo didn't give up. As Quasimodo lowered

us onto a large gargoyle, the judge swung at us with his sword.

"I should have known you'd risk your life to save that gypsy," he told Quasimodo coldly. "Just as your own mother died, trying to save you!"

"What?" Quasimodo gasped. Quasimodo had later told me that for twenty years he believed he had been abandoned, when the truth was much worse. Frollo had killed Quasimodo's mother even as she had tried to gain sanctuary in the cathedral!

While Quasimodo stood there, stunned by this news, Frollo tossed his cloak over Quasimodo. Quasimodo lost his balance and began to fall. But he managed to grab the end of Frollo's cloak and pull. Now it was Frollo who lost his balance and fell. Soon, Frollo dangled over the edge of the roof, clinging to his cloak for dear life.

Quasimodo held onto the end of the cloak with one arm, while clinging to the gargoyle with the other. They hung there for a moment. Fearing that Quasimodo would lose his grip, I reached down and grabbed his arm, trying to keep him from slipping.

"Hold on!" I cried.

But Frollo had managed to crawl up onto a nearby gargoyle. He was still holding his sword. As I clung to Quasimodo, Frollo chuckled as he raised the sword over me.

But at that moment, the gargoyle beneath his feet started to crack. Frollo let out a yell, scrambling for another foothold.

But it was too late! The gargoyle broke off,

sending the evil judge plummeting down, down, down to the square far below.

I hardly noticed—I was too busy trying to hold onto Quasimodo's hands. But he was just too heavy. My weak arms were no match for his weight. His hands started to slip out of mine. Quasimodo was going to fall!

At that moment, two strong arms reached out from a nearby balcony. It was Phoebus! He grabbed Quasimodo just in time, pulling him up over the edge of the balcony to safety.

We all hugged each other gratefully. I could hardly believe that the nightmare was over. Frollo was dead, and we were safe!

I gazed up at Phoebus's face. Just a short while earlier, I had been sure I would never look upon it again in this world.

 As we smiled at each other, I felt Quasimodo take my hand. He took Phoebus's as well. Then he joined them together. As he stepped away, Phoebus and I kissed.

A few minutes later, the three of us walked across the nave of the deserted cathedral. The light that filtered through the stained-glass windows created a golden glow on the marble floor.

The townspeople who had gathered in the square cheered when they saw us step into the doorway. We smiled at them gratefully. They were as happy about their freedom from Frollo's evil rule as we were. Best of all, they were all hailing Quasimodo as a hero.

I could tell that Quasimodo was a little nervous about all the attention. That wasn't surprising, considering what had happened the last time a crowd had cheered for him!

But this time, it would be different. As we stood there, a little girl broke away from the crowd and came forward. She stepped toward Quasimodo. For

a moment she seemed nervous, staring up at his misshapen features.

Then she dashed forward and wrapped her arms around him. Quasimodo smiled with wonder, leaning down to accept the little girl's embrace.

I smiled at Phoebus. At last, our friend would have his chance to live a good life outside the cathedral doors.

We stepped forward as the bells of Notre Dame

rang out above us. Moments later in the crowded square, I spotted a familiar, furry little face.

"Djali!" I cried, reaching out as the goat leaped toward me happily. I was so relieved that he was safe!

Then I danced through the celebrating crowd, greeting old friends and new ones alike. Everyone was filled with joy.

Still, I was glad when Phoebus found me a few minutes later and pulled me into a quiet corner. He put his arm around me, took my hand, and smiled down at me.

"Well, what do you think?" he asked.

I wasn't sure what he meant. "What do I think of what?"

"Of this. All this," he replied, waving a hand to indicate the crowds still celebrating nearby. "I mean, Quasimodo is a hero, your people are safe, Frollo is

gone forever, and the
battle is over. And
most important of
all, we can finally
be together."

I glanced out
at the crowds of
happy, faces. It made
my heart swell with
pride to see so many
of my people celebrating their freedom. Who could
have guessed that it could happen?

They say that Paris is the most modern of cities,
full of modern people with modern ideas. Perhaps
now, finally, we gypsies could be a part of it. Perhaps
now we could step out of the shadows and be proud
of who we were, just like my friend Quasimodo.

THE STORY OF
Belle

A Poor Provincial Life

The day began like any other—an ordinary day, typical of life in a small French village. The local farmer pushed a cart filled with plump orange pumpkins down the street. In a second-story salon, the barber began clipping his customer's hair. The butcher's stand opened for business, and his shouts rang out through the street. The pleasant smell of fresh fruit from the fruit seller's stand filled the air. All over the village, people opened their windows, breathed in the morning air, and called a cheery *"Bonjour!"* to their neighbors.

And as she did on most ordinary days, a young woman named Belle was walking toward the market. She was carrying a basket and looking at the everyday activities going on around her.

Most of the villagers knew the pretty brown-haired girl by sight. "Good morning, Belle," the baker greeted her as she passed his shop.

"Good morning, monsieur," Belle said politely.

The baker set a tray of freshly baked bread on his windowsill. "Where are you off to?" he asked Belle.

"The bookshop," Belle replied. "I just finished the most wonderful story about a beanstalk and an ogre and a—"

"That's nice," the baker interrupted. He leaned in the shop door to shout to someone inside. "Marie! The baguettes! Hurry up!"

Belle sighed and moved on, knowing the man wasn't really interested in hearing about her book. In this country town, most people weren't interested in fairy tales or stories of adventure. Of course, Belle wasn't like most people. She loved to read about anything. There were so many interesting things going on in those books! It was too bad the same couldn't be said for her village.

Luckily, there was a small bookshop in the marketplace. The owner allowed Belle to borrow books whenever she liked.

"Good morning!" Belle greeted the shopkeeper as she entered the bookshop. "I've come to return the book I borrowed."

"Finished already?" the shopkeeper exclaimed in surprise.

"Oh, I couldn't put it down," Belle told him. "Have you got anything new?"

"Not since yesterday," the storekeeper replied with a laugh.

"That's all right." Belle climbed the

ladder leading to the higher shelves. Spotting an old favorite near the top, she grabbed it. "I'll borrow this one."

"That one?" The shopkeeper peered at the cover through his spectacles. "But you've read it twice!"

"Well, it's my favorite!" Belle exclaimed. "Far-off places, daring sword fights, magic spells, a prince in disguise . . ."

The shopkeeper chuckled, charmed as always by Belle's enthusiasm. "If you like it all that much, it's yours! I insist!"

"Thank you, thank you very much!" Belle could hardly believe her good fortune. She and her father, Maurice, didn't have much money—her father was an inventor whose inventions only rarely worked—and so the gift of a book was something special.

Bidding farewell to the shopkeeper, Belle carried her new book out to the town square. As she wandered through the streets, her mind was far away. At first, she thought of the book she'd finished the night before, and then of the new one tucked in her basket.

Then her thoughts turned to her mother, who
had died when Belle was a little girl. It was through
her mother that Belle had come by her love of reading. Every night before bed, Belle's mother would
come to her daughter's room. Sometimes she would
bring a book she'd borrowed. At other times, she
would spin stories out of her own imagination. Even
in those days they hadn't had much money. But they
had always been happy. As soon as Belle was old
enough, her mother had taught her daughter to read
so that she could enjoy books on her own.

Soon after that, Belle's mother had taken ill and died. Belle and her father still missed her every day. But at least Belle could remember her through her own love of reading. Every time she read a new story, she imagined what her mother would think of it. That helped keep her mother's memory alive, just as much as the portrait sitting on Belle's dresser at home.

A Most Peculiar Girl

Sitting on the edge of the fountain in the town square, Belle turned through the familiar pages of her new book. She could hardly believe it belonged to her. She paused at her favorite part—the chapter in which the heroine meets her Prince Charming. It was such a wonderful story!

But she didn't have time to sit and read it just then. She wanted to get home to see how her father's latest invention was going. He had high hopes for this one. If he finished it in time, he

would be able to enter it in the fair being held the next day in a larger town a few miles away.

Still thinking about her book, she wandered back through town toward home. Partway there, a tall, handsome man dressed in hunting clothes jumped out in front of her.

"Hello, Belle," Gaston greeted her.

"*Bonjour*, Gaston," Belle replied politely. She didn't care much for Gaston—in her opinion he was vain, shallow, and silly, much more interested in improving his muscles than his mind. But that was no reason to be rude to the young man.

She prepared to move on, but Gaston had other ideas. Snatching the book out of her hands, he peered at it suspiciously.

"Gaston," Belle said with annoyance, "may I have my book, please?"

"How can you read this?" Gaston exclaimed. "There are no pictures!"

"Well, some people use their imagination." Belle couldn't help being amused by Gaston's simple-mindedness.

"Belle, it's about time you got your head out of those books and paid attention to more important things," Gaston declared, tossing the book into a mud puddle. "Like me!"

It was no secret that Gaston was interested in Belle. She was the prettiest girl in the village, and in Gaston's mind that made her the best. And he was sure that if anyone deserved the best, it was he! All

the other girls in the village swooned every time the handsome hunter walked by. Belle, however, seemed completely indifferent to his good looks. That only made Gaston all the more determined to win her over.

"The whole town is talking about it," Gaston went on as Belle knelt down to retrieve her book and wipe off the mud. "It's not right for a woman to read! Soon she starts getting ideas, and thinking. . . ."

"Gaston," Belle said, "you are positively primeval!"

Not realizing he'd been insulted, Gaston smiled. "Why, thank you, Belle! What do you say you and me take a walk over to the tavern and take a look at my trophies?"

"Maybe some other time," Belle replied.

Ignoring her refusal, Gaston put an arm around Belle and steered her in the direction of the tavern. Gaston was so unaccustomed to hearing anyone say no to him that he often didn't bother to take notice when someone did.

"Please, Gaston, I can't!" Belle managed to pull away after a few steps. "I have to get home to help my father. Good-bye."

Gaston's best friend, LeFou, stepped forward with a laugh. He had been watching the whole exchange.

"That crazy old loon?" he exclaimed at Belle's mention of her father. "He needs all the help he can get!"

Gaston laughed along with his friend. But Belle whirled around with an angry expression on her pretty face.

"Don't talk about my father that way!" she cried. "My father is not crazy! He's a genius!"

The blast of an explosion coming from the direction of her father's workshop interrupted any further discussion. Ignoring the two men's laughter, Belle ran for home.

When she got there, smoke was billowing everywhere. "Papa?" Belle called, coughing, as she entered the house and went down to the workshop. "Are you all right?"

"I'm about ready to give up on this hunk of junk!" Maurice cried in frustration.

Belle smiled, relieved to see that nothing was really wrong.

"You always say that," she reminded her father fondly.

"I mean it this time!" Maurice insisted. "I'll never get this boneheaded contraption to work!"

"Yes, you will," Belle assured him. "And you'll win first prize at the fair tomorrow. And become a world-famous inventor."

Maurice glanced at her. "You really believe that?"

Belle smiled at him. "I always have."

"Well, what are we waiting for?" Maurice asked, his good spirits revived, as always, by his daughter's support. "I'll have this thing fixed in no time!" He hurried back over to his invention. Belle stood by to hand him the tools he needed. "So, did you have a good time in town today?" he asked her.

"I got a new book," Belle said. But she wasn't really thinking about that. "Papa," she said uncertainly, "do you think I'm odd?"

"My daughter—odd?" Maurice exclaimed. "Where would you get an idea like that?"

"Oh, I don't know." Belle sighed, thinking of the conversation she had had earlier with Gaston. "It's just that I'm not sure I fit in here. There's no one I can really talk to."

"What about that Gaston?" Maurice asked as he fiddled with his invention. "He's a handsome fellow."

"He's handsome, all right," Belle said. "And rude, and conceited! Oh, Papa, he's not for me."

"Well, don't you worry," Maurice told her, "because this invention's going to be the start of a new life for us. I think that's done it." Making one last adjustment, he stood up. "Let's give it a try."

With a whir and a whistle, the invention came to life. Within moments it had chopped a log into firewood and tossed it neatly into a stack by the wall.

"It works!" Belle cried with delight.

"It does?" Maurice sounded surprised, then joyful. "It does!"

"You did it!" Belle exclaimed proudly, giving him a quick hug as more firewood flew through the air. "You really did it!"

Maurice asked Belle to hitch up his horse, Phillipe. "I'm off to the fair!" he declared.

Soon Belle was waving good-bye as her father  rode off with his invention in tow. She watched until he was out of sight, then wandered back inside. She wondered if her father was right. Would this invention really change their lives? Maybe now they would be able to get out of this sleepy little town and see the world!

In the meantime, she decided it was the perfect

moment to read her book. She went inside and picked it up.

For an hour or two, she was able to read in peace. Then there was a knock at the door. Belle looked up in surprise. Who could that be? She and her father didn't get many visitors.

Leaving her book open on the table, she walked over and checked the viewing tube—another of her father's inventions. It allowed her to see who was standing outside.

To her dismay, the tube showed her Gaston's smug yet handsome face. What in the world did *he* want?

Before she could decide what to do, Gaston pulled the door open and stepped inside. "Gaston!" Belle exclaimed. "What a pleasant surprise."

She didn't sound very convincing, but Gaston didn't seem to notice. Instead of wearing his usual hunting attire, he was dressed in a fancy coat and a jaunty tie.

"I'm just full of surprises," he said. "You know, Belle, there's not a girl in town who wouldn't love to be in your shoes. This is the day your dreams come true!"

"What do you know about my dreams, Gaston?" Belle asked with a rueful smile.

"Plenty!" Gaston assured her. He sat down in a chair beside the fireplace, comfortably propping his

muddy boots on the table—right on top of Belle's book. "Picture this: a rustic hunting lodge, my latest kill roasting on the fire . . ." He kicked off his boots, wriggling his toes. "And my little wife massaging my feet . . ."

Belle didn't try to hide her distaste as she stared at Gaston's ugly feet.

". . . while the little ones play on the floor with the dogs," he went on. "We'll have six or seven."

"Dogs?" Belle asked, still distracted at the thought of what Gaston was proposing.

"No, Belle," Gaston corrected. "Strapping boys, like me!"

"Imagine that," Belle said. Gaston had stood up by now, and Belle grabbed her muddy book and set it on the shelf before he could do any more damage to it. She had put up with just about enough of Gaston and his arrogance and self-centeredness. How could he assume that she would want to go along with his plans? It was obvious that he didn't understand her at all. And that was just as well, because she certainly didn't understand *him*!

Still, he kept talking. "And do you know who that little wife will be?" he asked teasingly.

"Let me think," Belle said nervously.

But Gaston wasn't interested in waiting for her to figure it out. "You, Belle!" he announced in reply to his own question. He leaned toward her, obviously expecting a thrilled response.

Belle slipped away. "Gaston, I'm—I'm—speechless!" She leaned against the front door, trying not to laugh out loud at the thought of marrying the crude hunter. "I really don't know what to say."

Gaston stepped toward her, leaning both hands against the door above her shoulders. "Say you'll marry me."

Belle gazed up at him. "I'm very sorry, Gaston," she said, feeling for the doorknob as Gaston pursed his lips and prepared to kiss her. "But— but—I just don't deserve you!"

And with that, she turned the doorknob and

stepped back. Gaston's weight pushed the door open, and he tumbled out, head over heels. "Whoa!" he cried as he splashed into a mud puddle outside.

Belle shut the door again quickly. She knew that Gaston had a temper, and she didn't want to face it right now. She was too annoyed herself.

Just imagine! A man like Gaston thinking that Belle would thank him for the chance to become his wife. It was outrageous. Preposterous. And it was just like Gaston to expect such a thing.

No, Belle had no intention of spending the rest of her life cooking and cleaning for that boorish, brainless man and taking care of a whole brood of wild children who took after their obnoxious father. She had much bigger dreams than that.

Including one very special dream . . .

SOMEDAY . . .

Belle couldn't help thinking back to something that had happened when she was young. It was just a year or two after her mother had died, soon after Maurice had moved their little family to the village. Belle had been thrilled the first time her father had taken her for a walk into the center of town. Everything was so different, so exciting!

"Look at this, Papa!" she had cried, racing ahead of him. She pointed to the fruit seller's stand—so many kinds of apples! And then to the fishmonger's

stand—all the different types of fish! To young Belle, life in this new town seemed wonderful.

It was a beautiful day in early spring. The villagers had smiled upon seeing the little girl's enthusiasm.

"What a pretty child!" A woman cooed, bending over to give Belle a pat on the head.

The woman's friend leaned toward Maurice as he hurried up to them, huffing and puffing from trying to keep up with his daughter. "You'd better keep a close eye on your little girl," she warned. "The gypsies are in town."

"Gypsies?" Belle cried with delight. "Mama read me a story about gypsies. They can see into the future!"

"Now, now, Belle," Maurice said with a chuckle, taking her by the hand. "That was just a story. Nobody can see the future."

The village women smiled and moved off. "Be careful," one of them called over her shoulder as Maurice and Belle continued on their way.

"Papa, can we go see the gypsies?" Belle begged, tugging on her father's arm. "Please, Papa?"

Maurice looked worried. "Well, I don't know, Belle," he said. "I'm not sure we should—ah!" Suddenly distracted, he pointed. "Look, Belle, a hardware shop! I'd better go see what sort of parts I'll be able to buy here for my inventions. Come along now."

Belle followed him into the shop. But she soon grew bored and restless. All there was to look at it in the hardware shop were bolts and hammers and rope. Through the window, she caught sight of a flash of bright color outside. What was that?

Slipping away toward the door, she glanced at her father. He was busy examining ax blades with the shopkeeper. Surely, he wouldn't mind if she just stepped outside for a moment. . . .

She was so busy looking over her shoulder that

she tripped over the door frame and fell right into a woman passing outside.

"Well, hello, little one," the woman said with a laugh.

"Oh, I'm sorry!" Belle gasped, righting herself and looking up into the broad, smiling face of a gypsy woman.

The gypsy laughed, making her golden hoop earrings jingle. "Don't fret, my child," she said kindly. "Such a little one as you could fall on me all day long without so much as ruffling my skirts."

Belle stared at the woman, fascinated. She looked so different, so interesting! "Can you see the future?" Belle blurted out.

The gypsy laughed again. "Well, now," she replied. "Why don't we just see about that? Give me your hand, child."

Feeling a little nervous, Belle held out her hand. What would the gypsy tell her? Would she predict a life of adventure and romance?

The gypsy peered down at Belle's little palm. "Ah,"

she said wisely. "You will live a long and happy life. But it will not always be easy. You will experience much adventure."

"Really?" Belle's eyes shone. "Adventure? That sounds wonderful!"

The gypsy gazed at her. "Remember this, my child," she said seriously. "Adventure is where you find it, and the true spirit of adventure lives only within your own heart. You must let it out by opening your mind."

Belle shivered. Hearing about the future was so exciting! "Tell me more," she begged.

The gypsy chuckled. "All right then, let's see." She looked at Belle's palm again. "Hmm, what's this?" she murmured, leaning over for a better view. "Odd. I've never seen this before. . . ."

"What? What is it?" Belle asked breathlessly.

"It looks like—well, it is a pattern that represents a castle," the gypsy said. "A great, gleaming castle of spires and towers. But the only castle like that around here is—"

"Belle!" Maurice's voice interrupted. He raced out of the shop and pulled her away from the gypsy. "There you are! You scared me half to death. Didn't I tell you to stay in the shop?"

"I'm sorry, Papa," Belle said, still thinking about what the gypsy had just said. "But listen! This lady was just telling me the most wonderful . . ."

Her words trailed off as she turned around. The gypsy had disappeared!

She convinced her father to search for her fortune-telling friend. They checked throughout the town, but the gypsy woman was nowhere to be found. Belle was left to wonder what else the woman might have said about her future.

Ever since that day, Belle had thought often about the gypsy's words. She thought about them again now as she ran away from the house toward a broad, grassy meadow with a stunning view of the river. There was a whole world of adventure out

there—she knew it. But here in her village, the only sense of adventure seemed to be in her heart, as the gypsy had said. There was certainly nothing exciting or new to be found in the everyday happenings of the village and its people. Even the feathery seeds of a dandelion blowing in the breeze seemed to have more adventures than Belle.

Someday I will go exploring, too, Belle told herself firmly. Someday I will have a life full of adventure. Then she sighed. Of course, it would be nice to have someone to share it all with, someone who really understands how I feel. . . .

A shrill neigh interrupted her thoughts. Glancing up, she was startled to see Phillipe racing toward her, still pulling her father's invention behind him. The horse's eyes were wide open and he seemed terrified.

And Maurice was nowhere in sight.

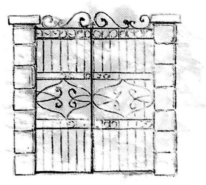

BELLE'S SACRIFICE

B elle hurried to the horse, taking him by the bridle and trying to calm him down. "Where's Papa? Where is he, Phillipe?" she cried. "What happened?"

Phillipe continued to stomp his hooves and shake with fear. Belle wished the horse could speak, to tell her what had happened to Maurice. What if there had been an accident?

She quickly unhooked the horse's harness and leaped onto his back. "We have to find him. You have to take me to him!"

Belle rode a good distance through the forest. The farther they got from the village, the darker it seemed to get. Then they reached a section where the trees were gnarled and shrouded in fog. Finally, Phillipe carried Belle to a huge iron gate set into a high stone wall. Beyond, Belle could see the twisted, dark outline of a huge castle.

"What is this place?" Belle murmured, staring at the castle with a twinge of fear.

Phillipe seemed more nervous than ever. Letting

out another snort, he started to rear up and back away.

"Phillipe, please, steady!" She soothed him. "Steady."

As Belle slid down from the saddle, she noticed something lying on the ground just inside the castle gates. She gasped as she recognized her father's hat.

"Papa!" she cried, pushing open the gate and grabbing the hat. She stared at it for a moment, then turned her gaze up to the forbidding castle. Could her father be in there?

Belle gulped, knowing she had to go inside. She took a deep breath and headed toward the castle. She crossed the drawbridge and soon reached the enormous front door. She pushed it open and peered inside.

"Hello? Is there anyone here?" Belle called.

A deep silence lingered in the vast, dark entrance way. The castle appeared to be completely deserted. "Hello?" Belle asked again.

Still, there was no answer. But Belle wasn't going to give up until she was sure that her father wasn't

trapped somewhere inside. She stepped toward the grand staircase at the back of the hall, and walked up the musty red-carpeted stairs.

"Papa? Are you here?" she cried.

The castle was spooky. Every footstep echoed, and Belle had the eerie feeling that she was being watched. But her concern for her father overcame her fear. She continued to search, moving up one cavernous hallway and down another, calling for her father all the while.

Finally, Belle reached the foot of a winding staircase leading into one of the high towers. Peering up the stairs, she spotted the glow of candlelight and heard a muffled sound, like that of moving feet.

"Hello?" she called, excited. Perhaps someone was here after all. Perhaps it was someone who knew where her father was! "Is someone here? I'm looking for my father!"

Belle climbed up the stairs. But soon she reached a nook, where a candle was burning, unattended.

Aside from the candle's flickering flames, there was no sign or sound of life.

"That's funny," she murmured under her breath. "I'm sure there was someone." She raised her voice. "Is anyone here?"

"Belle?" a weak but familiar voice replied from somewhere just above.

"Papa!" Belle raced up the last few steps. A torch was burning in a wall sconce, and she grabbed it as she passed, kneeling beside a barred cell.

Maurice reached out a hand toward her.  He was lying on the cold stone floor, looking frightened and miserable. "How did you find me?" he asked with a gasp.

"Oh, your hands are like ice!" Belle exclaimed as her father coughed. "We have to get you out of there!"

"Belle, I want you to leave this place!" Though still weak, Maurice's voice was urgent. "No time to explain. You must go. Now!"

"I won't leave you!" Belle cried.

At that moment, a strong hand clamped down on

her shoulder, pulling her away from the cell. Belle's torch went out as it tumbled to the floor. "What are you doing here?" a deep voice said with a growl.

"Who's there?" Belle cried. "Who are you?"

"The master of this castle," the voice replied from the shadows.

"I've come for my father," Belle said as bravely as she could manage. She peered into the darkness in the direction of the growling voice, but all she could see was a huge, shadowy mass. "Please, let him out. Can't you see he's sick?"

"Then he shouldn't have trespassed here!" The master of the castle roared back angrily. "He's my prisoner."

Belle argued with him, but soon she could see it would do no good. She knew what she had to do.

"Take me instead," she offered.

This time, the voice sounded surprised. "You would take his place?"

"Belle, no!" Maurice cried. "You don't know what you're doing!"

But Belle had made up her mind. "If I did, would you let him go?" she asked.

"Yes," the dark figure agreed. "But you must promise to stay here forever."

Forever? Belle gulped. What was she agreeing to, anyway? Who was this mysterious master of the castle? "Come into the light," she told him.

The figure hesitated. After a moment, he stepped forward into some light coming through a high, narrow window. Belle gasped in horror at the sight—an enormous, hideous beast!

"No, Belle!" Maurice cried. "I won't let you do this!"

That reminded Belle what was at stake—her dear father's life. She rose to her feet and approached the Beast. "You have my word," she told him.

"Done!" the Beast shouted.

Belle buried her face in her hands. What had she gotten herself into?

Meanwhile, the Beast dragged Maurice out of his cell. Maurice tried to convince Belle to change her mind. But before they could say more than a few desperate words to each other, the Beast pulled Maurice away.

"Wait!" Belle cried, but it was too late. She collapsed on the floor, sobbing. So much for her life of adventure! The rest of her life would be spent in this cold, gloomy cell.

A moment later, the Beast returned. He had just sent Maurice back to the village in his coach.

"You didn't even let me say good-bye!" Belle cried. "I'll never see him again, and I didn't get to say good-bye." She broke down into sobs.

The Beast didn't respond for a moment. Finally he spoke. "I'll show you to your room."

"My room?" Belle glanced up at him, confused. "But I thought—"

"You want to stay in the tower?" the Beast demanded. When Belle shook her head, he turned toward the staircase. "Then follow me."

He led Belle through the dim corridors of the castle. After a few minutes of silence, the Beast cleared his throat and spoke.

"The castle is your home now, so you can go any-where you like," he said. "Except the West Wing."

"What's in the West Wing?" Belle asked.

"It's forbidden!" the Beast roared.

Soon they reached a door. The Beast opened it and showed Belle inside. "If you need anything, my servants will attend you," he said as Belle stepped into her bedroom and looked around. "You will join

me for dinner," he added. "That's *not* a request!"
And with that, he slammed the door.

Belle collapsed onto the bed, feeling as if her
heart would break. How could she spend the rest of
her life here, the prisoner of that horrible, hateful
beast? And would she ever see her
beloved father again? After a few
minutes, a knock on the door and
a cheery voice interrupted Belle's
sobs.

"It's Mrs. Potts,
dear! I thought you might like
a spot of tea."

Belle gasped as a plump
little teapot hopped into the
room. She was so startled that
she backed into a wardrobe.

"Careful!" the wardrobe
sang out in a friendly voice.

Belle could hardly believe what
she was seeing and hearing. There

was Cogsworth, the mantel clock, who was the head of the household. Lumiere, the candelabrum, was the butler. Mrs. Potts, the teapot, and her son, Chip, the teacup, served in the kitchen. Even the castle's dog had been changed into a friendly, tassel-wagging footstool.

Meeting the kind, enchanted objects made Belle feel a little better. But she still had no intention of sitting down to dinner with the Beast who had imprisoned her.

The Beast was irate when he heard of her decision. "If she doesn't eat with me," he said, growling at the servants, "then she doesn't eat at all!"

A few hours later, Belle's stomach started to rumble. She decided to slip out of her room and look for something to eat. It didn't take her long to find the kitchen. Though Cogsworth was worried about defying the master's orders, Mrs. Potts,

Lumiere, and the others soon had all the kitchen objects working hard to fix Belle a delicious meal. They even sang and danced to entertain her while she ate.

As she finished the last course, Belle felt better than she had since coming to the castle. She decided to do a little exploring. Slipping away from Cogsworth and Lumiere, she crept up the staircase to the West Wing. What was there that the Beast didn't want her to see? She couldn't help being curious.

She found her way to a large, dark room with a balcony. It had once been beautifully furnished, but now it was a mess. There was a painting on the wall of a handsome young man. It appeared to have been ripped to shreds by huge claws. Had the Beast done that?

Belle stared at it for a moment, but then a strange reddish glow caught her eye. She turned and moved toward it. At the far end of the room, a door opened onto a balcony. Just in front of

the door was a table, and on that table stood a glass jar set over a beautiful, glowing red rose. The flower seemed to hang in midair as if by magic.

Stepping closer, Belle stared in awe. What was it? She lifted the jar for a better look.

At that moment, there was a roar of fury from behind Belle. Oh, no! The Beast had caught her snooping!

A Close Call

"Why did you come here?" the Beast growled, covering the red rose with its glass container and hunching over it protectively. "I warned you never to come here!"

"I—I'm sorry! I didn't mean any harm!" Belle stammered. As the Beast roared and started smashing things, Belle turned and raced for the door. His angry voice followed her all the way down the hall.

"Get out!" he howled.

Belle was terrified by the Beast's anger. She

raced for the front door, passing Cogsworth and Lumiere in the hall.

"Where are you going?" Lumiere cried.

"Promise or no promise, I can't stay here another minute!" Belle replied.

"Wait, please wait!" Cogsworth exclaimed.

But Belle didn't hesitate. She ran out through the door and found Phillipe in the stable. Moments later, they were galloping through the snow away from the castle.

It was past midnight, and the woods were dark and filled with shadows. After a while, Belle noticed nervously that some of the shadows seemed to be moving, even following her. She swallowed hard. Was she imagining things?

Then several sets of yellow eyes blinked into view, glowing in the dark of the underbrush. Belle gasped in horror as the creatures stepped forward into a clearing—wolves!

Phillipe reared up in panic as the wolves stalked toward him. Turning around, he ran for his life.

Belle clung to Phillipe's mane as he galloped through the snow with the wolf pack snapping at his heels. For a moment the two seemed to be out-running the pack, and Belle dared to hope that they might escape.

But several wolves had run ahead on another trail. As Phillipe crested a hill, some of the wolves darted out in front of him. Others were still coming from behind. They were surrounded!

As the horse reared up in terror, Belle was flung from the saddle. She dropped the reins, which got tangled up in the branches of a tree, so Phillipe couldn't move. The panicky horse kicked out at the wolves as Belle crawled to her feet. Grabbing a stout branch from the ground, she rushed to the horse's side and prepared to defend them both.

But as she glanced around, her heart sank. There

were so many wolves! How could she fight them all? It seemed hopeless.

Just as a wolf leaped at her, a roar rang out, louder than the growls of the wolves. A strong arm reached out and grabbed the wolf that was attacking Belle.

Belle gasped. It was the Beast! He must have followed her from the castle!

She watched fearfully as he fought the wolf pack. The animals attacked him fiercely, ripping at his

cloak and fur. But finally he overwhelmed them. Soon he had sent the last of them whimpering and fleeing into the night.

But the fight had taken all the Beast had. With a groan, he staggered and collapsed to the ground, unconscious.

Belle was already standing at Phillipe's side, ready to get back on. She paused, glancing back at the fallen Beast. For a moment she was tempted to

climb into the saddle and continue her ride toward
home—and her father.
With the wolves on the
run, there would be
nothing to stop her.

But she couldn't do it. She had no
idea why the Beast had fought so hard to save her,
but she couldn't leave him there to die.

She walked to his side and removed her cloak to
place it over him. Then she led Phillipe toward the
Beast's still body. It wasn't easy, but between the two
of them they managed to hoist the still, heavy Beast
over the saddle.

Then they began the long, slow trudge through
the snow back toward the castle.

When they arrived, the servants helped carry the
Beast into the parlor, where he soon regained consciousness in front of a roaring fire. Meanwhile,
Mrs. Potts and the others had brought hot water
and bandages so that Belle could clean the master's
many wounds.

Belle dipped a bandage in the hot water and squeezed it out. Looking up, she saw the Beast licking a deep scratch on his arm. "Don't do that," she chided. Ignoring the Beast's growl, she reached for his arm. "Just hold still. . . ."

The Beast roared in pain as the hot cloth touched his wound. "That hurts!" he bellowed so loudly that the servants took a step back.

But Belle didn't move away. "If you'd hold still, it wouldn't hurt as much!" she scolded him. After

what she'd just been through in the forest, somehow the Beast's shouts didn't scare her as much as they had before.

The Beast scowled at her. "Well, if you hadn't run away, this wouldn't have happened!"

"If you hadn't frightened me, I wouldn't have run away!" Belle retorted.

"Well, you shouldn't have been in the West Wing!" the Beast cried.

"Well, you should learn to control your temper!" Belle exclaimed.

For a moment, the two of them stared at each other stubbornly. Mrs. Potts, Lumiere, and Cogsworth glanced at one another in amazement. No one had ever dared to address the master that way!

When she spoke again, Belle sounded calmer. "Now hold still," she told the Beast. "This might sting a little."

Once again, she touched the hot cloth to the Beast's wound. He clenched his teeth in pain, but this time he kept quiet and still and let Belle do her doctoring.

Belle glanced up at him, realizing there was something she needed to say. "By the way," she said, "thank you for saving my life."

The Beast was surprised for a moment. Then he nodded, his expression softening slightly.

"You're welcome," he replied.

A Special Surprise

After a few days had passed, Belle found herself wondering why she had ever been afraid of the Beast. It was true that his looks were strange and frightening and his manners were a bit rough. But underneath the gruff exterior, he was also kind and curious and intelligent—even rather sweet.

One morning, he took her by the arm. "Belle, there's something I want to show you," he told her gently. He led her to a tall door in a part of the castle she hadn't explored yet. But before they entered, he turned toward her and said, "First, you have to close your eyes. It's a surprise."

Belle closed her eyes with a smile, wondering what he had in mind. She heard the door swing open, then felt his hands take hers as he led her forward.

"Can I open them yet?" she asked.

"No, not yet," he replied.

The Beast moved away, and Belle heard the sound of heavy drapes being pulled back. Even with her eyes closed, she could tell that the room had suddenly been filled with light.

"Now can I open them?" She had grown quite curious.

"All right," the Beast said—"now!"

Belle opened her eyes—and gasped in wonder. It was a library! An enormous, glorious, beautiful library filled with more books than she had ever

seen! Shelves stretched up to the ceiling high above, and tall, narrow windows illuminated the countless volumes that filled the room. Ladders and spiral staircases allowed access to the uppermost shelves.

Belle spun around, amazed and overwhelmed. She had never dreamed there would be so many books in the whole world! The contents of the little village bookshop would have fit into the smallest corner of the vast room.

"I can't believe it," she murmured. "I've never seen so many books in all my life."

"You—you like it?" the Beast asked.

"It's wonderful!" Belle cried.

"Then it's yours," the Beast told her.

"Oh!" Belle's head spun as she tried to take in the whole room. "Thank you so much!"

Slowly, the two of them were becoming friends. They were beginning to discover the joy of being together, and sharing things with each other. It was now pleasant for Belle to walk with the Beast in the snow-covered castle garden or go for a sleigh ride in the wintry forest. That first day, she never would have imagined that she would now be able to joke with him, that they could laugh so much together. The  enormous beast was so comical when he timidly held out his paw to feed the little birds in the garden. They didn't fear his horrible claws in the least, and neither did she—at least, not anymore.

And so their daily life continued happily, each day fading into the next. Belle realized she was actually quite content at the castle. The only thing she regretted was not knowing how her father was. She knew he must miss her terribly, as she missed him. If only she could see him again!

Still, she never regretted the promise she had made, especially now that the Beast had become so dear to her. And when he invited her to a special formal dinner, she accepted gladly.

 On the big day, Belle dressed carefully with help from Wardrobe. They chose a lovely golden gown

that set off her beautiful brown eyes and hair. When she came out of her room and walked down to the first landing of the staircase, she looked up. The Beast was standing there, gazing down at her.

She was a little startled by how handsome he looked. He was dressed in a dashing blue jacket with gold piping that matched her dress. His fur was clean and neat, and his gaze was hopeful and a little shy.

She smiled and took his arm as he reached her. They walked down the stairs together as music started to play. The servants had arranged every-thing to make the evening special—music, candle-light, and a delicious dinner. Belle and the Beast sat together at the dining table, enjoying their food and conversation.

As she finished eating, Belle was overcome by a

sudden urge. The music was so melodic, everything was so wonderful—she just couldn't resist. Pushing back her chair, she hurried over and took the Beast by the arm, asking him to dance.

He seemed surprised but pleased. Offering his arm once again, he led her into a grand ballroom. Glass doors all around offered a glorious view of the night sky filled with stars.

They danced. The music swelled around them, and Belle could feel her heart swelling, too. Being with the Beast made her so happy. Was this friendship, or was there some-thing more happening between them? She smiled, not certain of the answer. But there was plenty of time to figure it out.

When they were tired of dancing, the two walked out onto the terrace. The soft glow of the twinkling stars lit Belle's face as she gazed out at the night.

"Belle," the Beast addressed her uncertainly, taking her hands in his. "Are you happy here with me?"

"Yes," Belle responded immediately. But a moment later she glanced down, her contented expression turning a bit sad.

"What is it?" the Beast asked.

Belle hesitated only a moment before telling him the truth. "If only I could see my father again," she said. "Just for a moment. I miss him so much."

The Beast hated to see the pain in her eyes as she thought of her father. He had put that pain there by accepting her imprisonment in exchange for Maurice's. He couldn't quite regret the decision, as that was how he and Belle had come to know each other. Still, he wished he could do something to help her now.

Suddenly, he realized there *was* something he could do. The enchantress who had transformed him into a beast had left him with a couple of things. One was the magic rose—if he didn't learn to love another and earn her love in return by the time the last petal fell, he would be doomed to remain a monster forever. For a while he had been certain that the spell could never be broken. But lately, he had dared to hope that Belle might be the one to break it and change him and his servants back to their human forms.

The other item the enchantress had left behind was a magic mirror. For the many long years of his enchantment, it had been the Beast's only link to

the outside world. All he had to do was command it to show him something, anything, and that person, thing, or place would appear in the mirror's face.

"There is a way," the Beast told Belle softly.

He led her upstairs and picked up the mirror. Handing it to her, he explained, "This mirror will show you anything—anything you wish to see."

Belle stared at the mirror. Her own face stared back. Could it really work?

"I'd like to see my father, please," she told the mirror uncertainly.

The mirror glowed and sparkled. A moment later, instead of Belle's own reflection, the mirror showed a most upsetting scene.

Belle gasped as she recognized her father. He was lost in the forest, staggering weakly through the snow. He was coughing and she could see him fall to his knees.

"Papa!" Belle cried in dismay. "Oh, no! He's sick! He may be dying! And he's all alone!"

The Beast turned away when he heard the anguish in her voice. He gazed down at the magic rose, noticing that another petal had dropped. He caressed the glass jar, knowing that it wouldn't be long now. . . .

But he couldn't stand to

let Belle suffer a moment longer. Even if it meant sacrificing his own dreams, he must help her if he could. And he knew what he had to do.

"Then you must go to him," the Beast said.

His voice was so soft that Belle wasn't sure she'd heard him right. "What did you say?" she asked.

"I release you," the Beast said. "You are no longer my prisoner."

"You mean I'm free?" Belle was amazed. She had long since accepted that she would be here in the castle forever. But now the Beast was releasing her from that sentence so she could help her father. "Oh, thank you!" she told him, hoping he could hear in her voice how grateful she was for his kindness. "Hold on, Papa," she called out to the image in the mirror, even though she knew he couldn't hear her. "I'm on my way!"

She started to hand the mirror back to the Beast, but he pushed it gently away. "Take it with you," he said. "So you'll always have a way to look back and remember me."

"Thank you for understanding how much he needs me," Belle whispered, overcome with emotion. Now that she was free to go, she realized she had no desire to leave the Beast at all.

But she had to go. She had to save her father. Touching the Beast on the cheek, she turned away.

THE MAGIC MIRROR

Belle and Phillipe rode deep into the forest. The magic mirror guided the way, and it didn't take Belle long to find her father. She was just in time—he was lying unconscious in the snow, almost frozen.

Bundling him up, she helped him onto Phillipe and started for home. Soon she had him tucked into bed in their little cottage. With her tender care, he quickly regained consciousness.

"Belle!" he cried, hardly daring to believe it was really his beloved daughter looking down at him.

"It's all right, Papa," she assured him gently, dabbing his feverish face with a cool cloth. "I'm home."

"I thought I'd never see you again!" Maurice exclaimed.

Belle embraced him. "I missed you so much!"

"But the Beast!" Maurice suddenly remembered everything that had happened. "How did you escape?"

"I didn't escape, Papa," Belle told him. "He let me go. He's different now. He's . . . changed somehow."

She couldn't find quite the right words to

explain. Before she could think about it anymore, she heard a noise behind her. Glancing back, she saw Chip the teacup, popping out of her bag.

"Hi!" he said a bit sheepishly.

Belle laughed. "Oh! A stowaway!" she exclaimed.

Maurice laughed. "Why, hello there, little fella," he said, remembering how the little cup and his mother had been kind to him during his imprisonment. "Didn't think I'd see you again!"

Chip turned to Belle. "Belle, why did you go away?" he asked. "Don't you like us anymore?"

"Oh, Chip." Belle chuckled kindly. "Of course I do. It's just that—"

Before she could finish explaining, there was a knock on the door. Leaving Chip with her father, she went to answer it. Who could it be at this late hour?

Outside, she found a thin, pale old man with long white hair and an unpleasant expression. "May I help you?" she asked uncertainly.

"I've come to collect your father," the man said.
"Don't worry, mademoiselle. We'll take good care of
him."

The man stepped aside so Belle could see his
carriage parked out front. It was the carriage from
the local asylum.

Belle gasped. "My father's not crazy!" she
protested.

Suddenly, Gaston's friend LeFou stepped into

view. "He was raving like a lunatic!" he cried. "We all heard him, didn't we?"

Belle realized a crowd had been gathering beside the carriage. They cheered in agreement.

"No!" Belle cried. "I won't let you!"

Maurice had heard the commotion. He got out of bed and came to the front door. LeFou spotted him right away.

"Maurice!" he cried. "Tell us again, old man. Just how big was the Beast?"

As Maurice described the Beast, the crowd laughed in disbelief. Belle couldn't believe this was happening. They all thought her father was crazy. But he was telling the truth!

Before Belle knew what was happening, two order-lies stepped out of the carriage, grabbed Maurice, and dragged him away. "No!" Belle shouted. "You can't do this!" But she was powerless to stop them.

Suddenly, Gaston appeared. "Poor Belle," he said. He put his arm around her shoulder. "It's a shame about your father."

"You know he's not crazy, Gaston!" Belle cried, hoping he might be able to talk some sense into the other villagers.

"Hmm," Gaston said. "I might be able to clear up this little misunderstanding, if . . ."

"If what?" Belle prompted.

Gaston smiled slyly. "If you marry me."

"What?" Belle could hardly believe her ears. Now she was sure that Gaston was behind this. He had convinced the townspeople that Maurice was crazy—just to try to force Belle into marrying him!

"One little word, Belle," he urged. "That's all it takes."

"Never!" Belle exclaimed furiously, pushing him away in disgust.

Gaston scowled. "Have it your way," he said, walking away haughtily. He thought he was Belle's only hope. But he was wrong.

Belle ran back inside and grabbed the magic mirror.

"My father's not crazy, and I can prove it!" she cried to the onlookers. She held up the mirror. "Show me the Beast!" she ordered it.

The mirror glowed and changed. Suddenly, the Beast appeared for everyone to see.

He was howling out his misery

at losing Belle, and with her, all hope for happiness. While Belle could recognize his roaring as a cry of pain and sadness, the villagers were terrified.

"Is he dangerous?" someone cried out nervously.

"Oh, no, he'd never hurt anyone," Belle assured the crowd. "I know he looks vicious, but he's really kind and gentle. He's my friend."

Gaston scowled. "If I didn't know better, I'd think you had feelings for this monster," he said accusingly.

Belle was still furious about what Gaston had tried to do. "He's no monster, Gaston," she snapped. "*You* are!"

Gaston flew into a furious rage. "She's as crazy as the old man!" he sneered, grabbing the mirror from Belle. Then he whipped the townspeople into a frenzy of fear, telling them that the Beast would steal their children in the night and destroy the village if they didn't do something about him immediately.

"We're not safe until his head is mounted on

my wall!" Gaston declared. "I say we kill the Beast!"

The crowd let out a cheer. Belle tried to stop Gaston, but it was no use. He grabbed her by the arm.

"If you're not with us, you're against us!" he shouted. He ordered the crowd to lock Belle and her father in the basement of their house so they couldn't warn the Beast that the angry mob was coming.

Belle pounded helplessly against the basement door as she heard Gaston and his followers march off toward the castle.

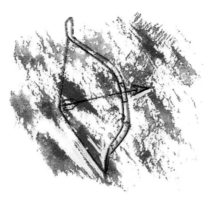

THE ATTACK

Belle was frantic. She pried at a window with a stick, but it wouldn't budge. This was all her fault!

"I have to warn the Beast!" she cried. "Oh, Papa, what are we going to do?"

"Now, now," Maurice tried to comfort her. "We'll think of something."

Luckily, little Chip was still upstairs. He went outside and peered at them through the window. He glanced nervously at the villagers marching away into the woods. As he watched them leaving, he noticed Maurice's woodchopping invention standing in the yard.

Suddenly, Chip had an idea. He managed to get the contraption moving! "Here we go!" he cried.

The ax at one end chopped at the air as it rolled down the hill toward the house. A moment later, it chopped right through the basement door, freeing Belle and Maurice!

Belle thanked Chip. Maybe now they had a chance to help save the Beast!

She and Maurice hurried outside, leaped onto Phillipe, and galloped off to the forest. Belle's heart pounded along with the horse's hooves. She had to warn the Beast! She knew that Gaston would stop at nothing in pursuit of his prey.

They rode through the darkened woods as fast as the horse could run. Would they get there in time? Belle urged Phillipe on.

Finally, the towers of the castle came into view. They rode through the gates and Maurice slipped off Phillipe's back. But Belle stayed in the saddle, staring up in horror. She had just seen the Beast, lying limply on one of the highest archways of the castle. Gaston was standing over him, a club held high over the Beast's head!

"No!" she cried.

The Beast heard her and stirred. When Belle had departed, he had been sure he would never see her again. Life hadn't seemed worth living. So when Gaston and his invaders had attacked, the Beast hadn't resisted.

But now everything had changed. She had come back!

"Belle!" the Beast murmured in wonder, hardly daring to believe she was really there. But as he lifted his head, he saw her in the courtyard below.

"No, Gaston!" she called desperately.

But Gaston paid no attention. He swung the club viciously, planning to end the Beast's life with a single blow.

But a strong arm shot upward, stopping the swing before it connected. The Beast suddenly had a reason to defend himself!

He leaped at Gaston with a loud roar. Gaston's face showed a flash of fear for the first time in his life. Then the fight was on!

Belle raced into the castle. She had to stop the two before they killed each other! She reached a balcony just above the fierce battle. She saw that the Beast had grabbed his rival by the throat and lifted him so that his feet dangled helplessly over the edge of a deadly drop-off.

Belle froze, unable to say a word. She watched as the Beast slowly pulled Gaston back to safety and dropped him on the ground.

"Get out," the Beast growled at Gaston.

"Beast!" Belle called to him with relief.

"Belle?" The Beast turned, his face lighting up with joy and wonder. He started to climb up toward her. "You came back!"

But while the Beast had shown mercy to Gaston, Gaston wasn't about to return the favor. He leaped up, pulled out a knife, and stabbed the Beast in the back!

The Beast fell back, and hung from the balcony railing. He howled in pain. But Gaston didn't have long to enjoy his victory. He lost his balance and fell, tumbling over the same drop-off the Beast had spared him from a moment earlier.

Meanwhile, Belle was hanging on to the Beast in desperation. With her help, he managed to climb up over the edge of the balcony, where he collapsed onto the ground.

Belle kneeled beside him, horrified. No! After all that had happened, the Beast couldn't die now!

The Beast opened his eyes. They were clouded with pain, but still his expression was happy as he gazed up at Belle. "You—you came back," he said again, gasping.

"Of course I came back," she replied, trying not to let her concern be heard in her voice. But it was no use. "I couldn't let them—" She broke down and

embraced him, her tears mingling with the rain that was falling. "Oh, this is all my fault. If only I'd gotten here sooner. . . ."

"Maybe it's better this way," the Beast managed to whisper.

"Don't talk like that!" Belle ordered him, her voice wavering. "You'll be all right. We're together now. Everything's going to be fine. You'll see."

She smiled weakly, trying to make herself believe it, too. The Beast smiled in return. It was a struggle to keep his eyes open, but still he gazed up at her. "At least," he said, gasping with enormous effort, "I got to see you—one last time."

With that, his eyes fell shut at last. "No!" Belle cried, feeling her heart break as his enormous body went limp. "No, please! Please don't leave me!"

She buried her face in his chest, sobbing as if she would never stop. How would she go on without him? She had just realized how important he really was to her.

"I love you," she whispered as she hugged his still body.

A Magical Moment

For a moment, Belle continued to sob over the Beast's body. She couldn't believe he was gone. It just wasn't fair. She had finally found true love, only to have it taken away from her. It was almost as if Gaston had won, after all.

Then, suddenly, a blinding flash of light whizzed past Belle, landing on the balcony.

Belle glanced up, confused, as another flash appeared, and another, and another until she and the Beast were surrounded by a glowing, sparkling light. She stared around in amazement.

The Beast's body started to move, floating up-ward as if lifted by invisible hands. Belle jumped back, startled. What was going on?

The Beast hung suspended in midair for a moment. Suddenly, Belle realized that he was changing in front of her eyes! His clawed hands transformed into smooth, pale human hands. His fangs turned into teeth. His fur became skin. He was changing from a beast into a man!

Belle was dumbfounded. What was happening? Where had her beloved Beast gone, and who was this handsome young man lying before her? She didn't understand.

Then the young man sat up and opened his eyes. He gazed at his transformed limbs in disbelief that soon changed to joy. Then he spun around and hurried toward her.

"Belle," he said in a soft, unfamiliar voice. "It's me!"

Belle gazed at him. Could it be? The voice, the face, the hair—it was all different. He looked nothing like the Beast.

But then she peered deeply into the young man's eyes. Yes, the eyes were familiar. They were the same eyes that had looked at her a few moments before with such tenderness and love! They wore the same expression now.

And with that, she dared to believe that what had happened was true. This *was* the Beast—changed back to his true human form.

"It *is* you!" she cried with joy. Her words of love had finally broken the spell!

Belle caressed his cheek, and he brushed the hair back from her forehead. Then he leaned down, and they shared their first kiss as more swirls of magical light surrounded

them, transforming the castle and all its servants back into their original forms.

If ever there was a reason to celebrate, this was it! Before long, Belle and her true love were dressed in their finery once again, dancing in the ballroom, surrounded by the happy servants of the castle. Maurice was there, too, thrilled to see his daughter so happy.

Belle was overjoyed as well. She had always dreamed of adventure and romance, and she had found both, more than she had ever imagined. And she had learned what the old gypsy woman had meant, too. She had learned to open up her heart. That was how she had seen the inner beauty beneath the Beast's hideous exterior, and grown to love him for who he was *inside*.

And now she would have a lifetime filled with joy to share with him. It was just like the happy ending in one of her books, only better—because this time it was real.

THE STORY OF
POCAHONTAS

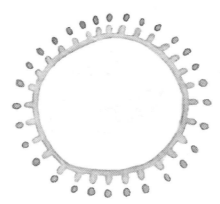

STRANGE CLOUDS

Pocahontas, the only daughter of Chief Powhatan, liked to go wherever the wind took her. With her constant companions, Meeko the raccoon and Flit the hummingbird, she explored the forests and rivers near her village.

One day, her father returned from an important battle, and wanted to find his daughter. But no one knew where she was.

Pocahontas's best friend, Nakoma, went searching for her. As she paddled her canoe down the Chicahominy River, she finally spotted Pocahontas standing on a high cliff, looking out over the river.

When Nakoma called out the news of Powhatan's return, Pocahontas smiled. Without hesitation, she dove down, down, down into the clear waters of the river. When she emerged from the water, she tipped her friend's canoe, dumping Nakoma into the river.

"Don't you think we're getting a little old for these games?" Nakoma sputtered.

In response, Pocahontas squirted a stream of water in her friend's face. Nakoma shrieked with

laughter and splashed her. Soon the two of them were having a water fight.

When they had tired of the game, the two friends righted Nakoma's canoe and climbed in. "What were you doing up there?" Nakoma asked.

"Thinking," Pocahontas replied as she squeezed water from her long, thick, dark hair.

"About the dream again?" Nakoma knew about the dream her friend had been having lately. Something to do with a spinning arrow . . .

But there was no time to think about that now. The two girls paddled quickly back to the village, where Powhatan was talking about the battle his warriors had just won.

"Our warriors fought with courage," he was saying as Pocahontas and Nakoma joined the crowd, "but none as bravely as Kocoum." He gestured to a stern young warrior standing beside him.

"Oh, he is so handsome," Nakoma whispered, watching as the tribe's medicine man painted Kocoum's broad chest with symbols of his bravery.

Pocahontas smirked. "I especially love his smile," she said. She respected Kocoum's strength as a warrior. But why did he always have to look so serious?

When the chief finished his speech, Pocahontas hurried to greet him. "My daughter!" Powhatan said when he saw her, reaching out for a hug. "Seeing you gives me great joy. Come with me. We have much to talk about."

Pocahontas walked with her father into a nearby longhouse. She was eager to tell him about her dream. He was so wise—perhaps he would be able to tell her what it meant.

"Father, for many nights now I've been having a

very strange dream," she said. "I think it's telling me something's about to happen. Something exciting!"

"Yes," Powhatan agreed with a smile. "Something exciting *is* about to happen. Kocoum has asked to seek your hand in marriage."

Pocahontas was startled at her father's words. "Marry Kocoum?" she said. "But he's so—*serious*."

Powhatan chuckled at her surprise. "My daughter, Kocoum will make a fine husband. With him you will be safe from harm."

"Father, I think my dream is pointing me down another path," Pocahontas protested.

"This is the right path for you." Powhatan knew that his daughter was a free spirit, just as her mother had been. But even free spirits had to settle down sometime. "Even the wild mountain stream must someday join the big river," he told her gently.

Pocahontas gazed out at the river. She understood what her father was saying. But she just couldn't imagine spending the rest of her life as Kocoum's wife. It seemed too safe, too easy. Too *boring*.

Her father pulled a beautiful shell necklace out of his clothes. "Your mother wore this for our wedding," he said, fastening it around his daughter's neck. "It was her dream to see you wear it at your own."

Pocahontas was too overwhelmed and confused to say another word to her father.

Later, Pocahontas and her animal friends sat by the river's edge. "He wants me to be steady like the river," Pocahontas murmured, staring into the water as it moved smoothly past the shore. Just then, a pair of playful otters began splashing around, and Pocahontas laughed at their antics. "But it's not steady at all! It's always changing. . . ."

She decided it was time to seek advice from the one creature even wiser than her father. So Pocahontas paddled down the Chicahominy in her canoe. When she reached a fork in the great river, she didn't go down the broad, smooth-flowing waters to the left. Instead, she turned down the right-hand fork, which twisted and turned over rocks and rapids as it flowed through a deep forest.

Soon Pocahontas was pulling her canoe into a

glade. There, a wise old spirit lived within a four-hundred-year-old willow tree. Her name was Grandmother Willow, and she had been like a mother to Pocahontas since the girl's own mother had died many years earlier.

As Pocahontas's canoe glided into the glade, the bark of the ancient willow's trunk formed into a kindly, wrinkled, smiling face. "Is that my Pocahontas?" Grandmother Willow  called out. "I was hoping you'd visit today. Why, your mother's necklace!"

"That's what I wanted to talk to you about." Pocahontas touched the necklace. "My father wants me to marry Kocoum."

"Kocoum?" Grandmother Willow said. She sounded surprised and slightly dismayed. "But he's so serious!"

"I know," Pocahontas agreed. "My father thinks

it's the right path for me. But lately I've been having this dream, and—"

"Oh, a dream!" Grandmother Willow exclaimed. "Let's hear all about it."

Pocahontas quickly described her dream. "I'm running through the woods," she said. "And then, right there in front of me is an arrow. As I look at it, it starts to spin—faster and faster and faster until suddenly it stops."

"Hmm." Grandmother Willow looked thoughtful. "It seems to me, this spinning arrow is pointing you down your path."

"But what is my path?" Pocahontas asked. "How am I ever going to find it?"

Grandmother Willow chuckled. "Your mother asked me the very same question."

"She did?" Pocahontas was surprised. "What did you tell her?"

"I told her to listen," Grandmother Willow replied. "All around you are spirits, child. If you listen, they will guide you."

Pocahontas did her best to do as Grandmother Willow said. She listened, opening herself up to any messages she might find in the earth, the trees, the water, the sky.

"I hear the wind," she said in wonder.

"Yes," Grandmother Willow said. "What is it telling you?"

"I don't understand. . . ." Pocahontas did her best to listen even closer to the breeze rustling the treetops. What was it saying?

"What does your heart hear?" Grandmother Willow asked.

Pocahontas closed her eyes and reached out with her heart, trying to hear the message she knew was out there. Suddenly, she understood the voice of the wind.

"It says something's coming—strange clouds?" she said.

She wasn't sure what that meant. But something told her to climb up into Grandmother Willow's top

branches. From there, she had a view over the tree-tops, all the way to the waters of the bay.

To her amazement, she saw billowing white shapes that looked like clouds floating over the ocean. Pocahontas couldn't take her eyes off the white shapes as they fluttered and danced in the breeze.

"Clouds," she murmured. She didn't know exactly what she was seeing, but a shudder ran through her. Yes, something was coming, just as her dream had predicted . . . something new and exciting—"strange clouds."

LISTEN TO NATURE

In the harbor, a group of adventurers from England surveyed the new land that lay before them. One of the sailors, a tall, handsome man named John Smith, led the way off the ship.

"Come on, men," he said cheerfully. "We didn't come all this way just to look at it."

Soon the men were busy tying the ship in its new port and unloading supplies. But John Smith wanted to get a closer look at the wilderness right away.

Meanwhile, Pocahontas had crept as close to the harbor as she dared. From her favorite overlook, she

watched as the tall man broke away from the group. In some ways he looked much like the men of her village. But he had unusual light-colored hair, and his clothes looked very peculiar to her.

Who was this stranger? What was he doing here? Pocahontas shrank back into the forest as the man climbed up the rocks, almost to the overlook. He surveyed the landscape with interest, but he didn't spot Pocahontas in her hiding place.

Meeko, curious like all raccoons, couldn't resist the temptation to get a closer look at the newcomer. With  an eager laugh, he scurried out toward the end of the overlook. Pocahontas tried to stop him, but he wriggled free.

The little raccoon leaped across to the tree where the man stood. He bumped into the man's boots.

John Smith was startled by the sudden thump against his legs. "Hey!" he cried, automatically drawing his knife.

He looked around, but didn't see an enemy anywhere. Finally, he looked down and spotted the raccoon at his feet. His face relaxed into a smile.

"Well!" he exclaimed. "You're a strange-looking fellow. Are you hungry?"

He pulled a few biscuits from his bag. Meeko sniffed at one suspiciously, then grabbed it and chewed it happily.

John Smith laughed. "You like it, eh?"

Pocahontas smiled as she watched. She didn't

understand the words this stranger spoke, but there was something about his face that she liked. She watched until a shout rose from below, calling the man back to his ship. Then she carefully and silently made her way back into the woods.

Meanwhile, at the village, the tribe was already discussing the newcomers. Kekata, the medicine man, had consulted the spirits, which had said that the strangers had weapons that spouted fire and would consume everything in their path. Worried about this new threat to his people, Powhatan had sent Kocoum with a scouting party to observe and find out more about the strangers.

Pocahontas was still watching the newcomers herself. She had made her way down through the woods closer to the beach. There, she had a clear view of the activity as the men planted a flag, unloaded more supplies, and began to set up a camp. The strange white shapes she saw approaching from the top of Grandmother Willow's tree were attached to these newcomers' ships!

Seconds later, she noticed the tall blond man glancing at the forest. He seemed very distracted from the work he was doing. Finally, he moved away from the others and entered the woods, clutching a long, thin sticklike object in his hands.

Pocahontas followed him, moving like a shadow from tree to tree. She could tell that the man was excited about the unfamiliar landscape around him. He climbed over rocks, swung from vines, and surveyed the tallest treetops.

Pocahontas smiled as she tracked him from cliff to valley to forest. He truly seemed to appreciate her beautiful home.

Finally, John Smith came upon a magnificent waterfall emptying into a clear river. He bent to splash his face with the cool, refreshing water. As he cupped water into his hands, he caught the reflection of movement in it. What was that? Something —or some*one*—was hiding in the trees on a rise behind him.

Instantly on guard, he glanced over his shoulder without moving his head. Who was there? Could it be one of the savages they'd expected to find in this wild land?

Pocahontas lost sight of the stranger as he moved away from the river's edge. She crept carefully down the rise, looking around. Where had he gone?

She stepped out onto the rocky shore, wondering how he had disappeared so suddenly. She had only taken her eyes off him for a moment. . . .

Meanwhile, John Smith was hiding behind the waterfall with his musket at the ready. He wasn't about to let a savage take him by surprise! By now he could see that the figure on the other side of the sheet of falling water was human, though he couldn't tell much beyond that.

When the figure stepped across to a rock just in front of where he was hiding, John Smith jumped out and aimed his musket. But he stopped short before firing, his jaw dropping in surprise. It was a woman—a beautiful young woman dressed in a deerskin garment, with flowing dark hair and deep black eyes!

Pocahontas stared at the stranger. A small part of her mind was ashamed for allowing herself to be seen. But most of her attention was focused on the man.

He was tall, as tall as the tallest warriors of her tribe. His eyes were blue, like the brightest ocean water. And what was that strange staff he was holding, pointing at her?

She wondered if it held magic, like the staff Kekata used at certain tribal ceremonies.

The two stared at each other in silence. After a moment, the man lowered his staff to the ground and stepped toward Pocahontas. She held her ground for a moment, watching him come closer.

Then, all of a sudden, she realized where she was. What was she thinking? She knew nothing about this stranger. For all she knew he could be a ghost or an evil spirit come to carry her off. Turning quickly, she raced toward the safety of the forest.

"No, wait!" John Smith called after her. He chased Pocahontas through the woods to another part of the river.

Pocahontas leaped into a wooden canoe she knew was docked there. As she prepared to push off from shore, John Smith skidded to a stop. He held out his hands to show he meant no harm.

"Please," he called. "Don't run off. I'm not going to hurt you."

He took a few careful steps forward. She gazed at him suspiciously, but didn't move.

He stretched out his hand. "Let me help you out of there."

She said a few words in a language he didn't recognize.

"You don't understand a word I'm saying, do you?" John Smith asked. Still, he held out his hand, palm up, hoping his body language would express his good intentions. As soon as he'd seen this beautiful young woman, he had wanted to know more about her.

Pocahontas stared at the fair stranger for a moment. His words were strange, but his meaning was clear. He wanted to help her from her canoe. Should she accept his offered hand? She had no reason to trust him, but something in his eyes made her stretch out her own hand.

As soon as their hands touched, the wind began to sing and swirl around them. Pocahontas heard a distant voice—Grandmother Willow's voice. *What does your heart hear?* she crooned.

Pocahontas's eyes widened. She stepped out onto the shore, still holding the stranger's hand. They looked into each other's eyes. The man spoke to her again, his words still sounding unfamiliar.

She closed her eyes, waiting for the wind to speak to her. Suddenly, she heard its message sweeping through her heart. The stranger was asking her a question: *Who are you?*

Opening her eyes, she answered him. "Pocahontas," she said simply.

"What?" John Smith was surprised to hear the young woman speak. "What did you say?"

"My name is Pocahontas."

John Smith was amazed. He had understood her! He wasn't sure how it had happened, but it was wonderful. "I'm John Smith," he said with a smile.

NATIVES

Pocahontas stared at the strange object on John Smith's head. It was made of a smooth and shiny material she didn't recognize.

"It's called a helmet," John told her.

"Helmet," Pocahontas repeated softly, savoring the sound of the new word.

The two of them were sitting on a grassy bluff overlooking the river. For the past few minutes, they had been getting to know each other. John had learned that Pocahontas was a daughter of the powerful tribe of Powhatan, whose people had lived on this land for many generations. In turn, John had shared some of his own background. He had explained that he and his shipmates had come from a far-off land across the sea, and that he loved to explore new lands. What he didn't tell her was that the leader of the expedition, Governor Ratcliffe, had already claimed the new land for the king of England, or that he planned to chase out any Indians he found while digging up the forest in search of gold. What would she say if she knew all that?

Not wanting to think about that anymore, he cleared his throat and looked out over the water. "So, what river is this?" he asked.

"Quiyoughcohannock," Pocahontas replied.

"You have the most unusual names here!" John said in amazement. "Chicahominy. Qui—Qui-yough-co-hannock. Pocahontas."

Pocahontas smiled shyly as he looked at her. "You have the most unusual name, too," she said. "John Smith."

At that moment, John noticed a little striped tail poking out of his bag. "Hey!" he cried, pulling out the same mischievous raccoon he had seen on the ridge over the harbor. "Is this bottomless pit a friend of yours?" he asked Pocahontas.

"Meeko!" Pocahontas chided, picking up the little raccoon.

"Well, how do you do, Meeko?" John offered his hand to the little creature.

Meeko grabbed it and peered at it, clearly hoping for some more biscuits.

Meanwhile, Pocahontas stared curiously at John's outstretched palm. Noticing her curious expression, he smiled.

"It's just a handshake," he explained. "Here, let me show you." He took Pocahontas's hand in his own and shook it up and down. "It's how we say hello."

"This is how we say hello," Pocahontas said. She raised one hand, palm facing forward, and traced a circle in the air. "*Win-gap-o*," she said in her own language.

"Wing-gap-o," John repeated, carefully copying word and motion.

"And how we say good-bye," Pocahontas went on, beginning to trace a circle in the opposite direction.

John Smith smiled and caught her palm with his own in midcircle. "I like 'hello' better," he said.

They stood smiling at each other for a moment, their hands resting against each other. They were interrupted by Meeko, who had just grabbed something else out of John's bag and raced off with it. This time it wasn't a biscuit, but a small, round item.

"What was that?" Pocahontas asked.

"My compass," John said. "It tells you how to find your way when you get lost. But it's all right—I'll get another one in London."

"London? Is that your village?" Pocahontas asked curiously.

"Yes, it's a very big village," he replied. "It's got streets filled with carriages, bridges over the rivers, and buildings as tall as trees."

Pocahontas couldn't imagine it. "I'd like to see those things!" she exclaimed.

"You will," John replied. "We're going to build them here. We'll show your people how to use this land properly." Now that he had come to know Pocahontas, he realized there was no need to chase her tribe off the land. He was sure these Indians would be able to live in peace with the new settlers. "We'll build roads and decent houses, and—"

Somehow, Pocahontas didn't seem excited about

the plans. "Our houses are fine," she interrupted.

"You think that," he assured her, "only because you don't know any better. We've improved the lives of savages all over the world!"

"Savages!" Pocahontas cried.

John tried to explain, but Pocahontas was angry with him now. How dare he come here, to her home, and insult her?

Still, she couldn't help wanting to help him understand. Just because her people were different from his, he thought that meant they were less civilized. She would just have to show him that wasn't true.

Taking him by the hand, she led him into the forest. If her own words were not enough to convince him, perhaps the spirits of nature, the voices of the wind and trees and water, could help her explain his error.

Mingling her voice with the songs of the earth, Pocahontas showed John a world he'd never realized was there—right in front of his eyes. She introduced him to the spirits that lived within everything, from an

ordinary boulder to the noble eagles soaring overhead.

He looked into the eyes of shy forest creatures—deer, otters, a playful bear cub—and saw them look back at him. He leaped headfirst from a waterfall, becoming part of its flow before splashing into the water below. He ran with Pocahontas down the hidden trails of the deepest pine forest and tasted wild berries warmed by the sun. As the sun set, he gazed up at the patterns of the stars overhead with new eyes.

For the first time, he began to understand that everything around him was a part of the intricate pattern of life on earth, from the vibrant young woman standing beside him to the copper-colored leaves blowing in the wind. Every living thing had its own spirit, from the tiniest sapling to the ancient sycamore towering overhead.

On that magical afternoon, lost in the eyes of a young woman who, just a short time before, would have seemed to him a savage, John Smith felt his heart beating to a new rhythm. He was finally learning to recognize the voices of the natural world all around him.

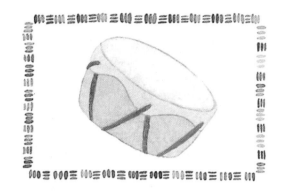

DRUMS OF WAR

Pocahontas was hardly aware of time passing as she and John Smith explored the forest together. But suddenly, she heard a distant, threatening sound through the trees.

"The drums," she said anxiously. "They mean trouble. I shouldn't be here."

John didn't understand. Why did she look so distressed all of a sudden? "I want to see you again," he said.

"I'm sorry. I have to go," Pocahontas murmured, racing off without a backward glance.

She ran home as fast as she could, worrying all the way about the drums—the drums of war. What did they mean?

When she reached the village, Nakoma told her everything. The chief had sent a party to spy on the strangers, but the spies had been seen. The pale men had attacked the warriors with strange sticks that spouted flames, and one of the tribe's finest warriors, Namontack, had been gravely injured.

That wasn't all. Before the attack, the warriors had seen that the newcomers were building a fort, cutting down trees, and digging huge holes in the earth.

Pocahontas was dismayed. Was this the help John Smith had spoken of? Did his people think they would help her people by wounding their warriors and cutting down trees?

Powhatan found his daughter and Nakoma gathering corn. "You should be inside the village," he told them.

"We're gathering food for when the warriors arrive," Nakoma explained. She had already told Pocahontas that Powhatan had called upon all the warriors of his allies' tribes to come to help them fight this new threat.

Powhatan nodded. "Don't go far," he warned. "Now is not the time to be running off."

"Yes, Father," Pocahontas agreed, though she couldn't help thinking of John Smith. Where was he now—with his own tribesmen, helping to dig up the earth?

"When I see you wear that necklace," Powhatan said gently, his grim expression softening, "you look just like your mother."

"I miss her," Pocahontas murmured, touching the shell pendant at her throat. If only her mother

were still alive—maybe she could advise Pocahontas what to do about her confusing feelings. Maybe she would understand her daughter's fascination with the strange man from over the sea.

"But she is still with us," Powhatan said with a smile. "Whenever the wind blows through the trees, I feel her presence. Our people looked to her for wisdom and strength. Someday they will look to you as well."

"I would be honored by that," Pocahontas said.

"You shouldn't be out here alone," the chief said to the two young women. "I will send Kocoum."

Pocahontas sighed as her father left. She had never felt so confused. It was as if she were being pulled in two different directions—toward the tribe she'd always honored and loved, and also toward the unusual new man who had captured her heart. She didn't know what she really wanted. But she certainly didn't feel like seeing Kocoum just then.

"All right, what is it?" Nakoma interrupted her thoughts. "You're hiding something." She had known Pocahontas a long time. She could tell something was troubling her deeply.

"I'm not hiding anything," Pocahontas insisted. Though she had shared many secrets with Nakoma, she couldn't tell her the truth this time. It would only get Nakoma in trouble.

Just then, the cornstalks rustled behind them. Nakoma gasped as John Smith stepped out. "Pocahontas, look!" she cried, her voice filled with fear. "It's one of them, I am going to get—"

Pocahontas clapped her hand over her friend's mouth. She stared at John. "What are you doing here?"

"I had to see you again," John replied.

"Pocahontas! Pocahontas?"

Pocahontas gulped. Kocoum was calling her from somewhere nearby. She had to get John out of there before the warrior saw him. "Please, don't say anything," she begged Nakoma quietly. Then she grabbed John's hand. "Quick, this way!"

She pulled him into the cornstalks seconds before Kocoum appeared.

THE COLOR OF GOLD

"This place is incredible," John said as Pocahontas led him across a natural bridge into the enchanted glade. Meeko and Flit came along, though Flit didn't seem happy that Pocahontas was bringing a stranger to this special place. The little hummingbird flew in and out of John's path, making it difficult for him to keep up. "And to think, we came all this way just to dig it up for gold."

"Gold?" Pocahontas said, not recognizing the word. "What's gold?"

"You know, it's yellow, comes out of the ground, it's really valuable," John replied.

"Oh!" Pocahontas reached into her bag. She pulled out one of the ears of golden corn she and Nakoma had been picking. "Here, we have lots of it. Gold."

John laughed and shook his head. "No, gold is . . . this," he said, pulling a coin out of his pocket.

"Hmm," Pocahontas said, examining the coin. "There's nothing like that around here."

Meeko grabbed the coin from her hand and nibbled it eagerly. When he realized it wasn't good to eat, he tossed it away in disgust.

John shook his head in dismay. "All this way for nothing," he said. "Well, those boys are in for a big surprise." He could imagine the look on Governor Ratcliffe's face when he heard the news. Ratcliffe was counting on this trip to make his fortune. Now it seemed there was no fortune to be found here.

"Will they leave?" Pocahontas asked. But what she really wanted to know was whether John would be leaving.

"Some of them might," he replied, lying back and staring up at the tree branches overhead.

Pocahontas had to ask the question in her heart. "Will you go home?"

John sat up. "Well, it's not like I have much of a home to go back to. I've never really belonged any-where."

"You could belong here," Pocahontas said softly.

The two of them gazed at each other for a moment. Then a soft breeze blew through the glade. John blinked. Was that—a voice? It sounded almost as if the wind itself were singing.

Suddenly, the old willow trunk in front of him shifted and formed an ancient-looking face. John stared, hardly believing his own eyes.

"What was that?" he exclaimed.

"Hello, John Smith." Grandmother Willow greeted him with a smile.

John gulped. "Pocahontas," he said, "that tree is talking to me."

"Then you should talk back," Pocahontas whispered.

"Don't be frightened, young man," Grandmother Willow said. "My bark is worse than my bite."

"Say something," Pocahontas urged John.

John looked uncomfortable. "What do you say to a tree?"

"Come closer, John Smith," Grandmother Willow said. John stepped forward, and soon the ancient tree spirit was staring directly into his eyes. "He has a good soul," she said after a moment. "And he's handsome, too!"

"Oh, I like her," John said with a chuckle.

Pocahontas laughed. "I knew you would."

"Smith! Smith, where are you, mate?"

The smile disappeared from John's face. He recognized the voices of his shipmates, Ben and Lon. "We can't let them see us," he whispered to Pocahontas, pulling her out of sight behind Grandmother Willow's thick trunk. "I'd better get back before they send the whole camp out after me."

"When will I see you again?" Pocahontas asked.

John turned and touched her cheek gently. "Meet me tonight," he said. "Right here."

After one last long look, he turned away and hurried back toward camp.

Pocahontas was left alone with Grandmother Willow. "What am I doing?" Pocahontas exclaimed, pacing back and forth. "I shouldn't be seeing him again. I mean, I *want* to see him again—something inside is telling me it's the right thing."

"Perhaps it's your dream," Grandmother Willow suggested.

"My dream," Pocahontas repeated thoughtfully. "Do you think he's the one the spinning arrow was pointing to?"

It was a new thought, and an interesting one. Pocahontas only wished she knew what it all meant.

RIPPLES IN THE WATER

As Pocahontas returned to the village a few minutes later, she saw a great number of warriors gathered on the shore of the river. More were arriving in canoes—her father's allies in other tribes had sent their warriors to help fight the new invaders.

Nakoma spotted Pocahontas. She looked terribly worried. "Pocahontas, are you crazy?" she cried. "What were you doing with—"

Before she could finish the sentence, Kocoum strode up to them. "There you are," he interrupted, sounding less stern than usual. "Look at them!" He put a hand on Pocahontas's shoulder and turned her toward the crowd of warriors. "Now we have enough warriors to destroy those white demons!"

Pocahontas could hear the excitement in Kocoum's voice. She guessed that he was looking forward to the coming battle. Her heart sank. How could she ever convince her people to talk of peace when they were already preparing for war?

She thought of John. For him, she had to try.

Spotting her father standing with the chief of one of the allied tribes, she hurried over to him. "Father, I need to speak with you."

"Not now, my daughter," Powhatan replied. "The council is gathering."

"We don't have to fight them!" Pocahontas cried as he turned away. "There must be a better way."

The chief turned back, his face solemn. "Sometimes our paths are chosen for us."

"But maybe we should try talking to them," Pocahontas suggested.

"They do not want to talk," he answered.

"But if one of them did want to talk?" Pocahontas asked desperately. "You would listen to him, wouldn't you?"

Powhatan sighed deeply. "Of course I would," he said. "But it is not that simple. Nothing is simple anymore."

Pocahontas watched as her father turned away and joined the council. Her father's words had given her a slight hope. She knew a man who would want to talk—to make peace with the tribe. When she met John that evening at the enchanted glade, the two of them would have to figure out a plan.

A little while later, as Pocahontas hurried away from the village through the cornfields, she heard a voice call out to her. She spun around. "Nakoma!" Pocahontas cried.

"Don't go out there," Nakoma warned. "I lied for you once. Don't ask me to do it again!"

Pocahontas turned away. "I have to do this."

"He's one of them!" Nakoma grabbed her friend by the arm.

"You don't know him," Pocahontas replied.

"If you go out there, you'll be turning your back on your own people," Nakoma said.

"I'm trying to help my people!" Pocahontas cried.

"Pocahontas, you're my best friend," Nakoma pleaded. "I don't want you to get hurt."

Pocahontas could tell that her friend was truly worried. But she could feel the time slipping away. She had to find John as soon as possible—everything depended on it! Nakoma would just have to trust her.

"I know what I'm doing," Pocahontas said, pulling away. She ignored Nakoma's cries as she ran into the tall forest of corn.

When Pocahontas reached the glade a few minutes later, Grandmother Willow was awaiting her anxiously. "The earth is trembling, child. What's happened?"

"The warriors are here," Pocahontas replied. There was no time to explain further, because suddenly John was standing beside her.

"Pocahontas," he said, his voice filled with worry. He grasped her hands in his own. "Listen to me. My men are planning to attack your people—you've got to warn them."

"Maybe it's not too late to stop this," Pocahontas said. "You have to come with me and talk to my father."

She began to drag him toward the village. But John held her back. "Pocahontas, talking isn't going to do any good," he said grimly. "I already tried talking to my men. But everything about this land has them spooked." He shrugged. "Once two sides want to fight, nothing can stop them."

"Now then, there's something I want to show you." Grandmother Willow's voice interrupted the tense moment. She lowered a long, slender branch toward the still water below. "Look."

The end of the branch touched the surface of the water, forming a ripple. The small circle of motion spread outward, becoming larger and larger.

"The ripples," Pocahontas said, seeing her point right away.

But John didn't understand so quickly. "What about them?" he asked.

"So small at first!" Grandmother Willow said. "Then look how they grow. But someone has to start them."

Finally, John understood what the ancient spirit was saying. But he didn't think it would work. "They're not going to listen to us," he said.

"Young man," Grandmother Willow chided, "sometimes the right path is not the easiest one. Don't you see? Only when the fighting stops can you be together."

On that point, John couldn't argue. He gazed down at Pocahontas, taking her hands in his own once again. He had to try—for her. Even if it

seemed hopeless, he and
Pocahontas had to try.

"All right," he said.
"Let's go talk to
your father."

Pocahontas was
overcome with
hope. With John
beside her, she could
help change her father's mind—she knew she could!
She flung her arms around him.

He hugged her back, then pulled away. They
stared into each other's eyes. Then their lips met,
and for a long moment everything else, even the
coming battle, faded away.

All of a sudden, a bloodcurdling war cry made
them jump. It was Kocoum! The warrior, filled with
rage, flung himself upon John.

"Kocoum! No!" Pocahontas cried as the two men struggled. "Stop!"

But before she could do anything, a shot echoed through the forest.

THE PRISONER

Kocoum grimaced in pain and toppled backward. He reached out to catch himself, but his hand locked onto Pocahontas's shell necklace. As he fell to the ground, the necklace came apart and broke into tiny pieces.

Pocahontas couldn't believe this was happening. But who had shot Kocoum? John was unarmed.

"Thomas!" John Smith cried as a frightened-looking young man ran out of the forest, clutching one of the pale men's strange war sticks.

Pocahontas fell to her knees at Kocoum's side. His

eyes were closed and his body was still. "You killed him!" she accused, glaring up at the newcomer.

Just then, the sound of many voices echoed through the forest. The Indian warriors were coming.

John gestured at Thomas. "Get out of here," he ordered, knowing that the young man was in grave danger.

Thomas hesitated, still looking terrified. He had thought he was protecting John against the Indians—

how could he have known it would cause so much trouble? Turning, he raced off into the forest.

Seconds later, the warriors arrived. They grabbed John and bound his arms behind him as Pocahontas watched helplessly, overwhelmed with guilt, confusion, and grief.

Back at the village, the moonlight outlined the faces of the Indians gathered around Kocoum's body. Powhatan's eyes were sad and grim.

"Who did this?" he demanded.

The warriors were dragging John toward the chief. "Pocahontas was out in the woods," one of the men said. "Kocoum went to find her, and this white man attacked him."

Powhatan approached John, who had been pushed to his knees in the clearing. "Your weapons are strong," the chief told the stranger. "But now our anger is stronger." He turned away to address his people. "At sunrise, he will be the first to die!"

Pocahontas stepped forward. She had to explain what had really happened. It was as much her own fault as it was John's! "But, father—" she began.

"I told you to stay in the village!" Powhatan interrupted, his eyes cold as he looked at her. "You disobeyed me. You have shamed your father."

"I was only trying to help," Pocahontas protested.

Her father would not listen. "Because of your foolishness, Kocoum is dead," he said.

Pocahontas sank to her knees as her father ordered the warriors to take John away. She stared at the ground, feeling hopeless. How had everything gone so terribly wrong?

A shadow fell across the ground. Looking up, she saw Nakoma standing before her.

"Kocoum was just coming to protect me," Pocahontas told her friend sadly.

"Pocahontas," Nakoma said, her voice choked with grief. "*I* sent Kocoum after you. I was worried about you. I thought I was doing the right thing!"

Pocahontas was startled by her friend's confession. But she was not angry. Like Kocoum, Nakoma had only had her best interests at heart. How could she blame either one of them for what had happened?

"All this happened because of me," Pocahontas said. "And now I'll never see John Smith again." She felt as if her heart were breaking.

Nakoma reached for her hand. She had let Pocahontas down once—she wouldn't do it again. "Come with me," she said.

A moment later, the two of them were standing before the prison hut. The warriors guarding the entrance looked at them in surprise.

Nakoma pushed her friend forward. "Pocahontas wants to look into the eyes of the man who killed Kocoum," she said firmly.

The warriors exchanged a glance. They knew the chief's daughter had a fiery spirit. Perhaps they shouldn't have been surprised to see her here.

"Be quick," one of them said, moving aside to let Pocahontas pass.

Pocahontas entered the hut. The interior was dark except for a moonbeam shining through the smoke hole in the roof. Its light revealed John Smith, who was bound to the center pole.

"Pocahontas!" he cried when he saw her.

"I'm so sorry," she whispered, overcome with emotion. She leaned against him for strength. "It would have been better if we'd never met—none of this would have ever happened!"

"Pocahontas, look at me," John insisted. He
waited until she met his gaze, then went on: "I'd
rather die tomorrow than live a hundred years without knowing you."

She gazed back at him, knowing that he spoke
the truth, because she felt the same way herself.
Even after all the terrible things that had happened,
and all that were to come, she couldn't truly wish to

change the past. She couldn't imagine going back to a time when she had not known John Smith.

"Pocahontas," Nakoma called softly from the door of the hut. The warriors were becoming impatient.

Pocahontas hardly heard her. She ran her fingers over John's face, her eyes memorizing its lines.

"I can't leave you," she said quietly.

"You never will," John replied with certainty. "No matter what happens to me, I'll always be with you—forever."

His calm courage gave Pocahontas strength. With one last caress, she stood and left the hut.

THE RIGHT PATH

"They're going to kill him at sunrise, Grandmother Willow," Pocahontas said, her voice filled with pain as she sat before the ancient tree spirit.

"You have to stop them," Grandmother Willow replied.

"I can't!" Pocahontas cried. How could she stop this terrible thing from happening? She hadn't even been able to convince her own father to talk to the newcomers. And now, she had shamed her father by talking to a settler on her own.

"Child, remember your dream!" Grandmother Willow encouraged.

Her dream—that was where all this tragedy had started. "I was wrong, Grandmother Willow," Pocahontas said. "I followed the wrong path. I feel so lost."

Even Pocahontas's animal friends, Meeko and Flit, were filled with sadness. They watched as she buried her face in her hands.

But suddenly Meeko brightened. Lost? He had heard that word before.

Racing for the hollow of an old tree trunk, the little raccoon rustled around in the goodies he had stashed there. Soon he found what he was looking for.

Pocahontas looked up as Meeko nudged something at her. What was it? She picked up the round, shiny object and stared at it.

"The compass," she said, wondering why Meeko had brought it to her. She remembered when the mischievous raccoon had taken it, and she hadn't seen it since. On one side, there were marks around

the edge of the circle. And in the middle was—a
spinning arrow! Pocahontas gasped in astonish-
ment.

"It's the arrow from your dream!" Grandmother
Willow exclaimed.

Suddenly, things didn't feel so hopeless after all. "I
was right!" Pocahontas cried. "It *was* pointing to
him!" As she stared at the compass, a beam of light
broke over the horizon. "Sunrise!" she said anxiously.

"It's not too late, child," Grandmother Willow

urged. "Let the spirits of the earth guide you. You know your path, child. Now follow it!"

Pocahontas knew her wise old friend was right, as usual. Springing into a run, she raced toward the village. The leaves of the trees seemed to part for her; the wind sustained her with invisible wings as she leaped from one rock to another. Still, she wasn't sure it would be enough. The rays of the morning sun grew stronger. Would she make it back in time?

At the same moment, Governor Ratcliffe was leading his men toward the Indian village, while Powhatan's warriors brought John Smith to the stone slab on the overlook. There, the execution would take place.

As one of Powhatan's men handed the chief his war club, another pushed John's head onto the slab. It was time to avenge Kocoum's death.

Powhatan raised the club. Below, he saw the new-comers emerge from the woods. They looked up, shouting angry words. But Powhatan didn't hesitate.

He raised the war club higher in the air, preparing to bring it down on John Smith's head with a killing blow.

Suddenly, Pocahontas appeared. She saw what her father was about to do. There was no time to call out to him, no time for reasoning. "No!" she shouted. With one last burst of energy, she ran forward and flung herself onto John's body, covering his head with her own.

Powhatan stopped in midswing, startled by his daughter's action. Pocahontas stared up at him defiantly.

"If you kill him, you will have to kill me, too!" she cried.

Powhatan frowned. "Daughter, stand back!" he ordered.

"I won't!" Pocahontas shouted. "I love him, Father."

Powhatan's eyes widened in surprise. Had he heard her right? Had his only daughter just claimed to love this stranger—this murderer?

In the valley below, the Englishmen had seen what Pocahontas had done. They murmured amongst themselves, wondering what was going on.

But Pocahontas paid attention only to her father. "Look around you," Pocahontas urged the chief. "This is where the path of hatred has brought us." She wrapped her arms more tightly around John's head. "This is the path I choose, Father. What will yours be?"

Powhatan looked around him. On one side, he saw the strangers holding their fire-breathing weapons at the ready. On the other side, his own warriors stood prepared to fight to the death for the tribe.

And in front of him, his daughter, his only child,

looked up at him with eyes full of strength and love.

At that moment, a gentle breeze blew up toward him from the valley, blowing through the trees and carrying their beautiful, multicolored leaves along in a dance of joy. He closed his eyes, listening for the spirit of his beloved wife. What was she telling him?

Suddenly, he took his club in both hands and

raised it high above his head. "My daughter speaks with a wisdom beyond her years," he announced. "We have all come here with anger in our hearts. But she comes with courage and understanding. From this day forward, if there is to be more killing, it will not start with me." He lowered the club and glanced at his men. "Release him."

Pocahontas smiled as the Indian warriors lowered their weapons. One of the men untied John's arms. She had done it! Now John would be safe.

"Fire!" a voice cried from below. It was Governor Ratcliffe—he still wanted to attack, even though the Indians didn't want to fight.

But his men had been affected by the scene they had just witnessed. They refused to raise their weapons.

"Fine, I'll settle this myself!" Ratcliffe grabbed a musket from one of the men. Raising it to his shoulder, he took aim at the chief standing on the overlook.

John Smith had his arms around Pocahontas.
Over her shoulder, he caught a glimpse of Ratcliffe
below. In a split second, he realized what the cruel
governor intended to do.

"No!" he cried. Leaping toward Powhatan, John
Smith shoved the chief out of the bullet's path—
putting himself directly in the line of fire.

Seeing what was happening, Pocahontas leaped
forward herself. But this time she was too late to
save John from harm. Her eyes widened in horror as
she saw his body jerk from the force of the bullet.

✳ ✳ ✳

Some time later, a pair of Englishmen were loading a dinghy with supplies to be sent out to the main ship. They looked up to see Thomas approaching. They knew he had been tending to John's wound.

"Is he going to make it, Thomas?" one of them asked.

Thomas sighed. "The sooner he gets back to England, the better." He knew that John was lucky to be alive at all. If he wanted to stay that way, he needed a doctor's care. "Is the ship ready yet?" he asked.

"Any minute now," one of the men replied.

Thomas nodded and returned to John, who was resting on a makeshift stretcher farther up the beach. "We'd better get you on board," Thomas told him.

"No, not yet," John said weakly. "She said she'd be here."

Thomas looked over his shoulder as he heard a sound from the woods. "Look!" he cried.

John lifted his head despite the pain. He saw a long line of people step out of the mist, all holding baskets of food and other supplies. At the head of the group was Pocahontas. As the others set down their gifts, she stepped forward.

Thomas spoke to Pocahontas as she passed him. "Going back is his only chance," he told her softly. "He'll die if he stays here." Then he and the others stepped away to give Pocahontas and John a moment alone.

Pocahontas kneeled beside John Smith. Suddenly, Meeko appeared beside her. He had something for her. Pocahontas couldn't believe her eyes.

"My mother's necklace!" The raccoon must have gathered up the pieces next to Kocoum's body and put them back together. Now it was like new.

Smiling at her little friend, she took it and fastened it around her neck where it belonged.

Then she turned her attention to John. He reached out to touch her face. "Come with me?" he asked.

It was the question Pocahontas had known was coming. She had been trying to decide what answer to give ever since she had learned that John needed to return to England to have his wound treated. But she still didn't know what to say. She glanced at her father, who had come with the others to see John off.

He smiled at her lovingly. "You must choose your own path," he told her.

Pocahontas looked at the two groups of people watching her. On one side of the clearing was the tribe

she had always known, and on the other was John's tribe, the Englishmen who had arrived so recently. Where did she belong? Which path was hers?

She knew her decision could be very important—not just for herself and John, but for their people as well. The two of them had helped stop the two groups from going to war, but that didn't mean the path to true and lasting peace would be an easy one. With John on his way back to England,

Pocahontas might be the best person to lead these separate peoples toward friendship. What would happen if she left now?

But what would happen if she stayed? She gazed at John. In the past few days, every angle of his face had become so familiar, so precious. How could she live without him? Was it selfish to want to remain at his side, no matter what the cost to anyone else?

Finally, she realized that her heart already knew the answer to that question. She gave her reply, knowing it was the true one. "I'm needed here," she told John softly.

"Then I'll stay with you," John said immediately.

"No," Pocahontas said, though her heart was breaking. "You have to go back."

"But I can't leave you," John told her.

"You never will," Pocahontas reminded him, thinking of the wise words he had spoken to her in the prison hut the night before. "No matter what happens, I will always be with you. Forever."

She kissed him one last time. Then she stood

and watched
as the
English
sailors lifted
the stretcher
and carried it to the
boat.

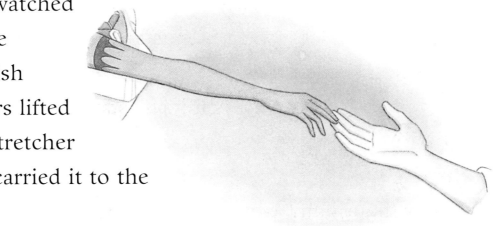

Powhatan approached
and put a hand on her shoulder. Pocahontas stood
with her father for a moment, taking strength from
his love.

Then she pulled away. As the English ship's
white sails caught the wind and the great vessel
moved out toward the sea, Pocahontas raced along
the shore, matching its progress, until she reached
the highest overlook. She stood there, her hair
blowing in the breeze, and watched as the strange
clouds carried John away.

On deck, John looked up and saw her. He raised
his hand, moving it in the circular motion that
Pocahontas had taught him.

Good-bye, he thought as he gazed up at her.

On the overlook, Pocahontas echoed the farewell gesture.

Good-bye, she thought as she watched the ship sail toward the rising sun on the far-off horizon.

THE STORY OF

Cinderella

HOPES AND DREAMS

It was almost dawn, and the sky over the horizon was beginning to change color. Cinderella was fast asleep in her room in the tower of the château where she lived with her stepmother, Lady Tremaine, and two stepsisters, Anastasia and Drizella. Her lovely face wore a happy smile, for she was dreaming of her childhood—back to the time when her dear father was still alive.

The house had been filled with love and laughter in those days. But there had always been a touch of sadness as well. Cinderella barely remembered her

mother, but she knew her father had missed his wife very much.

Sometimes Cinderella would see him gazing down at the pocket watch that her mother had given him the last Christmas they had spent together. "Are you feeling sad, Father?" Cinderella would ask, tucking her small hand into his.

He would always smile at the question. "How could I be sad?" he would ask as he swung her up into his arms. "I have the most beautiful little girl in the world as my daughter!"

Cinderella would hug him tightly. She adored everything about her father—his bright smile, his elegant clothes, his friendly manner, his handsome mustache.

In turn, the kind gentleman doted on his daughter. He provided her with the finest of everything, from clothes to toys to tutors. He often took her for carriage rides to see the King's palace, or to have a picnic by the river. He spent hours pushing her on the swing in the garden, telling jokes until she was giggling so hard she could hardly hold on to the swing's ropes. She couldn't imagine a better life than living with him in the château.

But her father wasn't so sure that their life was truly complete. He felt that his daughter needed a mother's care. That was the reason he proposed marriage to a local widow, Lady Tremaine. She was a handsome woman from a good family, with two young daughters of her own—he was certain she would be the perfect stepmother for Cinderella.

"I think this is best for all of us, my dear," Cinderella's father told her. "You will have a mother again. And little Anastasia and Drizella will be the sisters you never had. How does that sound?"

"Wonderful, Father," Cinderella replied.

Though she knew she would have to get used to sharing her dear father with the newcomers, Cinderella really didn't mind the idea of the marriage. She hoped that having a new wife would make her father less lonely. Perhaps it would even make her own life better.

At first, that wish seemed to come true.

"What a beautiful child!" Lady Tremaine cooed upon meeting her new stepdaughter for the first time. "Such lovely golden hair, and such a pleasant face! Why, I don't remember ever meeting a young lady so charming."

"Thank you," Cinderella responded politely, curtsying just as her father had taught her. She noticed that Anastasia and Drizella were scowling at her, but she didn't worry about that. She was sure they would all be the best of friends before long.

For a while, life at the château was as pleasant and calm as ever. At first, Cinderella tried to befriend her new stepsisters. But Anastasia and Drizella were more interested in shopping for new dresses or gossiping about the goings-on at the King's palace than they were in playing in the garden with Cinderella. And so Cinderella continued playing alone or with her father. But even though Cinderella's new stepsisters were rather foolish and vain, their mother always treated her stepdaughter kindly. So Cinderella was happy.

Everything changed

the day that Cinderella's father died unexpectedly. It was only then that Lady Tremaine's true nature was revealed. Freed from her husband's watchful eye, she showed herself to be cold, cruel, and bitterly jealous of Cinderella's sweetness and beauty. She was determined to provide the best life for her own daughters, but their awkward manners and homely appearance were only magnified beside Cinderella's charms. So Lady Tremaine did all she could to dull those charms. She forced Cinderella to dress in plain peasants' clothes, live in a tiny, drafty room at the top of the tower, and wait on her stepfamily hand and foot, night and day.

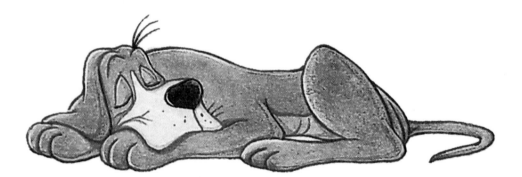

Sometimes Cinderella felt she had no friends left in the world, aside from her father's old dog, Bruno, and the little mice that lived in the walls of the house. Still, she never lost her kind, generous nature. And she never gave up her dreams of being happy again someday.

MORNING CHORES

A maidservant's day begins early, and that was what Cinderella had become—a maidservant in her own home. Awakening to the sweet songs of the birds outside her window, Cinderella yawned and stretched.

"Cinderella!" one little bird chirped.

The other flew through the open window and perched on the bed. "Cinderella!" it twittered.

Cinderella sat up, smiling at the birds. She scolded them playfully for spoiling her pleasant dream. The birds chirped back in protest and flew over to the window to show her the rising sun.

"Yes, I know it's a lovely morning," Cinderella told them, reaching back to undo her long, blond hair from its nighttime braid. "But it was a lovely dream, too."

Still, she knew that morning had to begin some-time, and it was nice to wake up to the beautiful voices of songbirds. In return, she sang to the little birds—as well as some mice that crept out of their holes to listen—as she brushed her hair.

The toll of a clock interrupted her sweet song. Cinderella looked out her window, which framed a view of the King's palace in the distance, including the clock tower.

Cinderella frowned slightly. "Oh, that clock," she said. "Old killjoy! Come on, get up, you say. Time to start another day."

The mice and birds watched sympathetically as Cinderella got out of bed and slipped on her shoes. She looked at them with a wistful smile.

"Even *he* orders me around," she said, gesturing to the clock. "Well, they can't order me to stop dreaming."

Still humming under her breath, Cinderella went about her morning routine. With a little help from her animal friends, she made the bed and got dressed. The birds tied a clean apron around her waist, Cinderella pulled back her hair in a tidy ribbon, and then she was ready to start the day.

In truth, Cinderella had never liked to sit around

with nothing to do, and she was always happy to keep busy. Deep down, the house still felt like home, and she didn't mind doing her part to take care of it. But why did she have to do everything? Why did Anastasia and Drizella have new gowns every season, while Cinderella was forced to make do with a few worn old garments? Why did the sisters spend  their days with music lessons and needlepoint, while Cinderella spent hers preparing meals, doing laundry, and scrubbing floors?

Still, she tried not to think about such things too much. She had learned long ago that it was easier to do as she was told rather than resist her lot in life. When the chores were done promptly and well, her

stepfamily left her alone—usually. They were busy enough with their own problems. Anastasia and Drizella had reached a marriageable age, and Lady Tremaine was determined to find them suitable husbands. It wasn't an easy task, however. The two girls had grown from awkward, demanding, and unpleasant little girls into awkward, demanding, and unpleasant young women. Was it any wonder that suitors were nowhere to be found?

Still, Lady Tremaine refused to give up, doing all

she could to make her daughters more eligible, from hiring the finest tailors to make their clothes to teaching them the arts and skills young ladies of their class should know.

Cinderella made her way down the winding tower staircase to the second-floor hallway, opening the drapes to let in the morning sunlight. She moved as quietly as possible, knowing that her stepmother and stepsisters were still sleeping.

Tiptoeing to one of the doors in the hall, she cracked it open. Inside, her stepmother slept in a huge canopy bed. Beside the bed was an elaborate little bed where Lady Tremaine's fat black cat, Lucifer, slept. He was curled up there now, snoring contentedly.

"Here, kitty, kitty," Cinderella called softly.

Lucifer heard her. Opening his sly green eyes, he looked at the girl in the doorway. He stood, stretched—and lay down again with his back to her.

Cinderella frowned. It was easy to lose patience

with the stubborn, selfish cat. "Lucifer!" She snapped. "Come *here*!"

The cat scowled. But he knew better than to disobey—at least before breakfast. Jumping down from his bed, he slunk out the door after Cinderella.

"I'm sorry if Your Highness objects to an early breakfast," Cinderella told him as she led the way toward the stairs. "It's certainly not my idea to feed you first."

Downstairs, she poured a bowl of milk for the cat  and greeted Bruno the dog, who was sleeping on the kitchen rug. Then she walked outside to the stable yard.

"Breakfast time, everybody up!" she called out. "Hurry! Hurry!"

She tossed out grain for the chickens. The mice popped out of their holes, and songbirds fluttered down from the eaves, eager for their share. Cinderella always made sure there was extra food for her little

friends, even though she knew her stepmother wouldn't approve. Sometimes it was convenient to be the only one who paid attention to the workings of the household!

Meanwhile, Lucifer had left his breakfast and was stalking one of the mice, a chubby little fellow named Gus. The cat watched, his tail twitching, as Gus struggled to pick up several kernels of corn and carry them back to his hole. Finally, Lucifer pounced, trapping Gus behind a broom in the corner. Aha! He had the mouse right where he wanted him. . . .

But the other mice weren't going to let Lucifer

catch their friend. When they pushed over the broom, it conked Lucifer on the head as it fell. That gave Gus enough time to race inside and hide under one of the teacups Cinderella had set out for breakfast.

Cinderella didn't notice the cat's antics. She was too busy worrying about the time as she tried to get everything done. It was getting late—if she didn't hurry with the breakfast, her stepfamily would wake up before she got there, and then—

"CINDERELLA!"

"All right, all right!" Cinderella raced over to the table. "Goodness, morning, noon, and night . . ."

"CINDERELLA!" another shrill voice rang out.

"Coming, coming," Cinderella muttered, though she knew her stepmother and stepsisters couldn't hear her. Gathering up the three breakfast trays, she headed up the stairs.

A Busy Morning

As Cinderella entered the first room in the upstairs hallway, she didn't realize that poor little Gus was still hiding under one of the cups on her trays.

"Good morning, Drizella," Cinderella greeted her sleepy stepsister pleasantly. "Sleep well?"

Drizella responded with a grunt. "As if you cared!" she added crossly. Then, she pointed to a large pile of wrinkled clothes on the floor. "Take that ironing and have it back in an hour. One hour. Do you hear?"

Cinderella set down one of the trays and picked up the clothing with her free hand. "Yes, Drizella," she said with a sigh.

She moved on to the next doorway. Once again, she walked inside and set down one of the breakfast trays.

"Good morning, Anastasia," she said politely.

"Well, it's about time!" Anastasia responded in a huff. "Don't forget the mending. And don't be all day getting it done, either!"

"Yes, Anastasia." Once again, Cinderella exchanged the tray for a basket of clothes. Then she left and headed for her stepmother's bedroom.

Lady Tremaine was sitting up in bed, waiting for her breakfast. Cinderella hesitated in the doorway, a little intimidated by her stepmother's stern expression.

"Well, come in, child," Lady Tremaine said. "Come in."

"Good morning, Stepmother," Cinderella said softly.

Lady Tremaine didn't return the greeting. "Pick up the laundry and get on with your duties," she said coldly.

"Yes, Stepmother," Cinderella said, setting down the final tray and picking up a third basket of clothes.

As she returned to the hall, a scream rang out from the second doorway. "Mother! Oh, Mother!" Anastasia screeched.

A moment later Anastasia burst into the hall, still dressed in her nightgown. She pointed an accusing finger at Cinderella.

"*You* did it!" she shrieked. "You did it on purpose! A big ugly mouse under my teacup!" She raced into her mother's room.

Cinderella immediately looked for the cat. She spotted him crouched near the doorway. "All right, Lucifer," she said. "What did you do with him?"

She reached down and picked up the cat, releasing Gus, who had been trapped under Lucifer's paws. The little mouse scooted away between Cinderella's

legs, heading for the nearest mouse hole, where he celebrated his freedom with his friends.

But Cinderella knew there was more to come. Sure enough, her stepmother's voice rang out a moment later—"Cinderella!"

Cinderella reluctantly returned to her step-mother's room. Anastasia and Drizella smirked as she entered.

"Are *you* going to get it!" Anastasia taunted.

Cinderella tried to explain that she hadn't hidden

the mouse there on purpose, but her stepmother wouldn't listen. Instead, she punished Cinderella by assigning her extra chores.

"The large carpet in the main hall—" she said with a hiss. "Clean it! And the windows, upstairs and down—wash them! Oh, yes, the tapestries and the draperies—"

"But I just finished—" Cinderella interrupted in protest.

Lady Tremaine didn't let her continue. "Do them again!" she cried. "And don't forget the garden, then scrub the terrace, sweep the halls and the stairs, clean the chimneys, and of course there's the mending and the sewing and the laundry."

Cinderella slumped under the weight of her stepmother's words. How could one person be expected to do so much? But she didn't argue. She knew it wouldn't do any good. Instead, she got to work.

It wasn't easy getting everything done, especially when her stepsisters kept interrupting with extra tasks. As Cinderella was sweeping the kitchen floor,

Anastasia burst in. She was holding her embroidery hoop. "Cinderella, these dumb old threads keep getting tangled," she complained. "Fix them for me!"

Cinderella sighed and reached out for the hoop. It wasn't that she minded helping—she knew that Anastasia was hopeless with a needle. But she would have minded less if her stepsister ever said a simple "please" or "thank you."

"Here you go," she said, quickly untangling the threads. "If you hold them to one side with your free hand, they shouldn't get tangled as easily."

Anastasia grabbed back the hoop. "I certainly don't need any tips from *you*," she snapped. "What do you know about embroidery? Or anything that has to do with being a proper lady?"

Turning up her nose, Anastasia stalked out of

the room. Cinderella merely sighed and went on with her work.

A little while later, Cinderella walked down the hall, carrying a load of laundry. She heard muttering coming out of the parlor. When she glanced inside, she saw that Drizella was standing at her easel with a paintbrush in her hand.

"What are you looking at?" Drizella said sourly. "Go away."

Cinderella started to move on. But suddenly Drizella called her back.

"Wait!" she yelled. "Get in here. I can't get the right shade of blue for the sky in my painting. Mix it for me— and make sure it's right."

"I'll try," Cinderella said, taking the tubes

of paint from her stepsister. She quickly added a bit of cloudy white, then a smidge of ocean blue, until she had created a perfect azure blue summer sky.

She dabbed a bit of the paint on Drizella's canvas and stared at it. Oh, to be out having a picnic under a clear blue sky, thought Cinderella.

Cinderella didn't realize her stepmother had entered the room until she heard her clear her throat. "That doesn't look like the laundry soap you're holding, Cinderella," Lady Tremaine said coolly.

Cinderella dropped the paint palette, startled. "I—I'm sorry, Stepmother," she stammered. "I was just—"

"She was just trying to ruin my painting!" Drizella interrupted. Snatching the canvas off the easel, she shoved it in front of her mother. "See? She smudged up the whole sky! It will never look right now!"

"Never mind, Drizella," Lady

Tremaine said. "I'll see that Cinderella works off the cost of a new canvas. But now, it's time for your music lesson. Come along."

"Oh, Mother," Drizella whined. "Can't we just skip music lessons today?"

Lady Tremaine frowned. "Not if you want to become a proper young lady, suitable for a rich husband to marry," she said. "Now come along—let's find your sister."

As they swept out of the room, Cinderella bent to clean up the paint. She hated her stepsisters' music lessons—they filled the whole house with their screeching—but at least they would be busy for a while. Maybe now she could catch up on her chores.

A ROYAL INVITATION

A few minutes later, Anastasia and Drizella were in the music room in the middle of their lesson. Anastasia blew a shrill, off-key tune on the flute, while Drizella attempted to sing along. Their mother accompanied their song on the piano.

Cinderella winced as she listened from the hallway, where she was scrubbing the marble floor. Who knew two people could hit so many wrong notes in such a short period of time?

Still, she managed to recognize the song her

stepsisters were trying to perform. It was one of her favorites—her father had often asked her to sing it for him. Cinderella hummed along, her melodious voice mingling with the tuneless screeches coming from the music room.

She scrubbed in time to the song. Somehow, the music seemed to make the work go faster. Soap bubbles floated up from her bucket, filling the air with their bright, weightless shapes, catching the light and reflecting beautiful rainbows of color.

Cinderella could see her own reflection in them—a girl in an apron, on her hands and knees,  scrubbing the floor. Soon, she started to daydream—she was dressed in a beautiful gown adorned with sparkling jewels, dancing beneath a canopy of stars. . . .

Then the pleasant dream burst just as suddenly as one of the bubbles when she noticed Lucifer crossing the room. His muddy feet left dirty tracks all over her nice clean floor. The cat paused and glanced at her with a smug, satisfied look.

"You mean old thing!" Cinderella cried. "I'm going to have to teach you a lesson." She chased the cat out of the room with her broom.

Just then, Cinderella heard a knock at the door. Before she could open the door, she heard a voice from the other side.

"Open in the name of the King!"

The King! Cinderella was surprised and curious. She swung open the door and saw a smartly dressed messenger standing outside. He held out an

envelope
sealed with
red wax.

"An urgent
message from
His Imperial
Majesty," the
messenger
announced.

Cinderella
curtsied as

she accepted the letter. "Thank you," she told the messenger.

Then she shut the door and looked at the envelope. What could the message be? She couldn't imagine, but it was wonderfully exciting to receive such a letter!

Deciding that something this important shouldn't wait, she rushed to the music room and knocked on the door.

"Yes?" her stepmother's voice snapped from within.

Cinderella entered the room, still holding the royal letter.

"Cinderella!" Lady Tremaine said with a frown. "I've warned you never to interrupt us."

"But this just arrived from the palace," Cinderella told her.

"From the palace?" Drizella exclaimed, rushing toward Cinderella. "Give it here!"

Anastasia was right beside her. She shoved her

sister out of the way and snatched the letter. "Let me have it!" she cried.

"No!" Drizella wailed. "It's mine! You give that back!"

Lady Tremaine stepped forward. "*I'll* read it," she announced, taking the letter from her daughters. As all three girls watched, she opened the envelope and scanned the letter. "Well," she said. "There's to be a ball."

"A ball!" Anastasia and Drizella cried in delight.

"In honor of His Highness, the Prince," Lady Tremaine went on. "And by royal command, every eligible maiden is to attend!"

"Hey, that's us!" Drizella exclaimed.

Anastasia nodded. "And I'm *so* eligible!"

Cinderella stood dumbfounded as her stepsisters continued to ooh and aah over the news. A ball? She knew of the prince, of course. He had been traveling recently, but she had overheard her stepsisters gossiping and knew that he was due to return to the kingdom any day now. She had also heard them say that the old King was eager to see his only son settled down and married as soon as possible.

Cinderella had heard that the Prince was very handsome, and very kind. What would it be like to meet him, perhaps even dance with him? She couldn't imagine it, and

until a moment ago wouldn't have dared to try. But the letter had said *every* eligible maiden. . . .

"Why," she cried, "that means I can go, too!"

Drizella laughed. "Ha!" she exclaimed. "Her, dancing with the Prince?"

Anastasia gave a mock bow, pretending to be Cinderella. "I'd be honored, Your Highness. Would you mind holding my broom?"

With that, she and Drizella burst into scornful laughter. Cinderella frowned.

"Well, why not?" Cinderella asked. "After all, I'm still a member of the family. And it says, by royal command, every eligible maiden is to attend."

Her stepmother glanced down at the letter, her face impassive. "Yes, so it does," she said. "Well, I see no reason why you can't go." She looked at Cinderella, ignoring her own daughters' expressions of dismay. "*If* you get all your work done."

"Oh, I will!" Cinderella cried, hardly believing her good luck. "I promise!" She dashed toward the door, eager to get started so there would be no chance of missing out on the royal ball.

"*And,*" her stepmother cautioned, "if you can find something suitable to wear."

Cinderella beamed at her. "I'm sure I can." She still had a trunk of her mother's old dresses up in her tower room. Surely, there would be something in there that would be suitable. "Oh, thank you, Stepmother!"

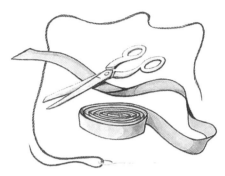

THE PERFECT GOWN

Even though there were still plenty of chores to be done, Cinderella couldn't resist hurrying up to her room to look in her mother's old trunk. She opened it and dug through the contents. Just as she remembered, there were several dresses inside—including a beautiful pink- and- white ballgown. It was a bit out of style, but the fabric was clean and in good condition.

She swung the dress around to show it to her little mouse friends, who had gathered nearby to watch. Holding it up to herself, she smiled at them.

"Isn't it lovely?" she said. "It was my mother's." She turned and pulled the gown onto the dressmaker's dummy standing against a wall in the room.

 "Well, maybe it is a little old-fashioned," Cinderella added. "But I'll fix that."

Cinderella had always been quick and skilled with a needle and thread. Recently, she had been forced to use her skills to maintain the wardrobes of her stepmother and stepsisters. All that practice had made her fingers even more agile and swift. Now, finally, she would have a chance to sew for herself!

 She grabbed her sewing basket. There was a book inside that showed all the latest fashions. "There ought to be some good ideas in here," she murmured happily.

Flipping through the pages, Cinderella found exactly what she wanted. "This one!" she cried.

The mice looked at the picture. They chattered excitedly, approving of her choice.

"I'll have to shorten the sleeves," Cinderella mused, as she stood up and started dancing around her room. "I'll need a sash—a ruffle—and something for the collar, and then I'll—"

"Cinderella!"

The distant cry interrupted her thoughts. She frowned in the direction of the door. "Oh, now what do they want?" she exclaimed.

"Cinderella! Cinderella!"

Cinderella sighed and touched the soft fabric of the dress. "Oh, well," she said. "Guess my dress will just have to wait."

As she hurried out of the room, the mice chattered amongst themselves. Though Cinderella didn't seem to realize it, they could see what was happening. Cinderella's stepmother claimed she would let her stepdaughter attend the ball—*if* her chores were finished and her dress was ready. But the mice were sure that Lady Tremaine would never really allow Cinderella to go to the ball. She would be too likely to outshine her plain stepsisters! Instead, the mice were certain that Lady Tremaine planned to pile on the chores until there was no time left for Cinderella's own sewing.

It just wasn't fair! The mice were determined to help their friend if it were at all possible.

And they had a very good idea about how they could do it. . . .

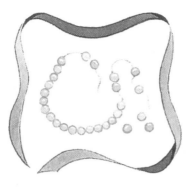

GETTING READY

When Cinderella returned, Anastasia and Drizella were already busy choosing their outfits for the ball. Somehow, though, none of their gowns seemed to be suitable. And as usual, that meant more mending, washing, and sewing for Cinderella.

"Cinderella, take my dress!" Drizella ordered, tossing a gown at her stepsister.

Anastasia rushed over with an armful of clothes. "Here, mend the buttonholes," she said, adding to Cinderella's load.

"And press my skirt," Drizella continued, piling on more. "And mind the ruffles, you're always tearing them!"

"And Cinderella," Lady Tremaine added, "when you're through, and before you begin your regular chores, I have a few little things . . ."

Cinderella felt her heart sink as she added up all the time it would take to do the things her stepfamily was demanding. How was she supposed to finish all these extra chores and still have time to prepare for the ball herself?

Unfortunately, she didn't have any choice but to

obey. She would just have to work as quickly as possible and hope for the best. "Very well," she whispered, turning away.

She spent the rest of the day rushing from the laundry room to the kitchen, back to the laundry room to the barn as fast as her legs would carry her! She hemmed her stepsisters' gowns, fixed their lunch, and rescrubbed the floor—thanks to Lucifer. The more chores she finished, the more it seemed she still had left to do. She didn't entirely give up hope until the sun set and she heard the clip-clop of horses' hooves outside.

Glancing out a window, she saw a fine carriage pulling up to the house. Lady Tremaine had hired it to pick up the family and drive them to the palace for the ball. Trying not to let her disappointment show on her face, Cinderella knocked on the door of the room where her stepmother was helping her daughters get dressed.

"The carriage is here," she said, without looking her stepmother in the eyes. How naive she had been! She had truly believed that her stepmother wanted to let her go. When in fact, she realized now, there had never really been any chance at all.

"Why, Cinderella!" Lady Tremaine feigned surprise. "You're not ready, child."

"I'm not going." Cinderella stared straight ahead. Whatever she did, she would not cry in front of them. She would never let them see how much they'd hurt her.

"Oh, what a shame," Lady Tremaine responded smoothly as her daughters smirked at each other. "But of course, there will be other times, and—"

"Yes," Cinderella cut off her stepmother's words. She couldn't stand to listen anymore. And she certainly didn't want to hang around and watch her stepfamily set out for the ball. "Good night."

It took all of her energy to drag herself up the stairs to her attic room. Instead of enjoying a wonderful, magical evening, dancing at the ball, talking to people, maybe even meeting the Prince, she was doomed to another lonely night in the attic, with only the mice as company. It wasn't fair! If her father were still alive . . .

But no. She couldn't think about that, or she really would break down and cry. That part of her life—the happy part—had ended long ago. She had no choice but to accept it.

Closing the door behind her without lighting the lamp, she wandered across the room toward the window. In the deepening twilight, the palace shone like a shimmering jewel lit from within.

"Oh, well, what's a royal ball?" she murmured, trying to make herself feel better. "After all, I suppose it would be frightfully dull. And—and—boring. And—and—" She sighed, giving in to the urge to feel sorry for herself. "—and completely wonderful."

 Seconds later, she turned and gasped in amazement. Her dress! But how—who—?

The gown was hanging from her dressing screen. The skirt had been draped with a silk sash and adorned with bows and ruffles. The sleeves had been shortened to look more stylish. Another bow decorated the neckline, which was now trimmed in lovely pink ribbon. It was beautiful!

"Surprise!" the mice cried in their squeaky voices. They jumped up and down, very pleased with  their efforts. It had been difficult finding all the trimmings—especially when Lucifer could be lurking around  any corner. But it was all worth it to see the amazed expression on Cinderella's face.

"Why, I—I never dreamed—it's such a surprise!" she stammered, grabbing the dress and holding it up, admiring it in the mirror. "How can I ever— why—oh, thank you so much!"

There was no time to say anything more. Cinderella quickly changed into the beautiful gown and ran a brush through her blond hair. The mice helped fasten a string of beads around her neck. It was the perfect finishing touch!

Then Cinderella raced down the stairs, calling "thank you" to her little friends over and over again. Soon she was dashing into the hall. Her stepsisters and stepmother were preparing to head outside, where the coach was waiting.

"Now remember," Lady Tremaine was telling her daughters. "When you're presented to His Highness, be sure to—"

"Wait!" Cinderella cried, interrupting. "Please, wait for me!"

She skidded to a stop in front of her family. Beaming, she spun around to show off her dress.

"Isn't it lovely?" she said breathlessly. "Do you like it? Do you think it will do?"

For a moment, Anastasia looked stunned. Then she looked angry. "Cinderella!" she cried.

Drizella joined in. "Mother," she whined, "she can't!"

"Girls, please." Lady Tremaine silenced her daughters with a look. "After all, we did make a

bargain, didn't we, Cinderella? And I never go back on my word."

As Anastasia and Drizella pouted, their mother peered more closely at Cinderella's dress. Cinderella smiled uncertainly. Shouldn't they be leaving? She didn't want to be late to the ball. But she remained silent under her stepmother's scrutiny.

"Hmm," Lady Tremaine said after a second. "How very clever, these beads." She touched the necklace Cinderella was wearing. "They give it just the right touch." She turned and glanced pointedly at her daughters. "Don't you think so, Drizella?"

"No, I don't," Drizella began angrily. "I think she's—" Finally getting a good look at the beads, she interrupted herself with a gasp of annoyance. She had just recognized the necklace as one she had discarded earlier that day. "Oh, why you little thief! They're my beads! Give them here!"

Cinderella gasped as her stepsister grabbed at the beads, ripping them off her neck. "Oh, no!" she cried.

"Oh, and look!" Anastasia exclaimed. "That's my

sash!" Darting forward, she tore the sash right off the front of Cinderella's dress.

"Oh, stop! Please!" Cinderella was horrified—she didn't know where to turn, what to do. How could they be so cruel? She tried to get away, but it was no use. Her stepsisters continued ripping her beautiful dress until it was in tatters.

Finally, Lady Tremaine spoke up. "Girls," she

scolded. "That's quite enough. Hurry along now—both of you. I won't have you upsetting yourselves."

Anastasia and Drizella obeyed, stepping haughtily out the door. Lady Tremaine followed, pausing just long enough to glance down at Cinderella, who was standing, staring down at the remains of her gown in shock.

"Good night," Lady Tremaine said pleasantly before exiting after her daughters.

As soon as she was alone, Cinderella broke down, burying her face in her hands. She raced outside, hardly knowing where she was going. She just wanted to get away—away from this house, from her terrible stepfamily, her awful life. How had she ended up so miserable? She had tried to be a good person, to remain cheerful. She had tried to hold on to her dreams. But what good had it done, after all?

Reaching the garden, she collapsed against a bench and sobbed. Finally, after all these years, they had done it. They had truly broken her spirit.

BIBBIDI-BOBBIDI-BOO

For several long moments, Cinderella wept hopelessly. For once, she couldn't even imagine feeling happy again. She couldn't find a way to believe that things would get better.

"It's just no use," she whispered aloud. "No use at all. I can't believe—not anymore. There's nothing left to believe in—nothing!"

"Nothing, my dear?" a friendly voice asked.

Cinderella paused between sobs. Who had spoken? She'd thought she was all alone here in the garden. Suddenly, she realized that her head was no longer resting on the cold, stone bench, but was cradled in a soft, comfortable lap.

"Oh, now, you don't really mean that," the voice went on.

"Oh, but I do," Cinderella said, looking up into the kind, wrinkled face of an older woman. The woman was dressed in a blue hooded cape, and her eyes twinkled with wisdom and merriment.

"Nonsense, child," the woman responded cheerfully. "If you'd lost all your faith, I couldn't be here. And here I am!"

Cinderella wasn't sure what to think. Who was this woman? What was she doing here?

Meanwhile, the woman stood and helped Cinderella to her feet. "Come now, dry those tears," she said. "You can't go to the ball looking like that."

Cinderella glanced down at her torn dress. "The ball?" she said. "Oh, but I'm not . . ."

"Of course you are," the woman said briskly.

"But we'll have to hurry, because even miracles take a little time."

Cinderella blinked. "Miracles?"

The woman nodded, but she seemed a bit distracted. She glanced around. "What in the world did I do with that magic wand?" she murmured. "I was sure I—"

"Magic wand?" Cinderella repeated in amazement. Suddenly, everything was beginning to make sense—the old woman's sudden appearance here in the quiet garden, the twinkling, wise eyes, the magic wand . . . "Why, then you must be . . ."

The woman glanced at her. "Your Fairy Godmother, of course," she said, as if it were the most ordinary thing in the world. "Now, where is that wand—oh! I forgot. I put it away!"

She waved her hand in the air. Just like that, a wand appeared in a cloud of magical sparkles.

Cinderella gasped. So it was true! This really *was* her Fairy Godmother! She stood, speechless with wonder, as the woman gazed at her thoughtfully.

"Now, let's see," the Fairy Godmother murmured. "Hmm. I'd say the first thing you need is . . ."

Cinderella glanced down at her tattered dress.

". . . a pumpkin!" the Fairy Godmother cried.

"A pumpkin?" Cinderella said in confusion. She glanced over her shoulder at the pumpkin growing in the garden.

The Fairy Godmother ignored her consternation. She was tapping her chin, thinking hard. "Now, uh, the magic words," she mumbled. Suddenly, her face brightened. She cleared her throat and blurted out a bunch of strange syllables. Cinderella couldn't follow any of it except the last three words: "Bibbidi-bobbidi-boo!"

At the same time, the Fairy Godmother was

pointing her wand at the pumpkin. Magic sparkles shot toward the pumpkin—and with a shudder and a jump, it transformed into an elegant, gleaming coach!

"Oh!" Cinderella gasped. "It's beautiful!"

Several of the château's animals had crept out to see what was going on, including the mice, Bruno the dog, and the old horse from the stables. Even Lucifer had wandered out of the house to investigate the commotion.

Next the Fairy Godmother pointed at the coach. "Now, with an elegant coach like that, of course, we'll simply have to have . . ."

The horse stepped forward eagerly. But the Fairy Godmother wasn't looking at him. She pointed her wand again.

". . . mice!"

She waved her wand over a group of startled mice as she sang out the magic words once again. When she had finished, the plain little mice were transformed into four gleaming white horses!

Lucifer was so startled that he fell into the fountain with a splash.

"Ha-ha, poor Lucifer," Cinderella said with a smile.

"Serves him right, I'd say," the Fairy Godmother replied. "Now, where were we? Oh, goodness, yes. You can't go to the ball without a . . ."

Cinderella smiled. Maybe now she would take care of her dress!

". . . a horse!"

"Another one?" Cinderella said in surprise.

This time, the Fairy Godmother pointed her wand at the old horse. Tonight he wouldn't need to pull the coach—he would sit in the driver's seat and hold the reins! Soon he had been transformed into a uniformed coachman. A moment later, Bruno, too, had been called into service. He would be the footman.

With that done, the Fairy Godmother seemed satisfied.

"Well, well, hop in, my dear," she said to Cinderella. "We can't waste time."

"But, uh . . ." Cinderella gestured to her torn dress. "Don't you think my dress . . ."

"Yes, it's lovely, dear," the Fairy Godmother said distractedly. "Lov—" Suddenly she gasped. "Good heavens, child! You can't go in that!"

Cinderella sighed, smiled, and shook her head.

The Fairy Godmother got ready to go back to work. "Now, let's see, dear," she murmured, stepping toward Cinderella. "Your size—and the shade of your eyes—something simple, but daring, too . . ."

She took a deep breath and, once more, said the magic words. Cinderella held her breath. She could feel magic flowing around her, and she could see it, too—twinkling like fireflies. She closed her eyes as it washed over her.

When she opened them again, she looked down and gasped. "Oh!" she cried. "It's a beautiful dress!"

And indeed it was. It was made of yards and yards of flowing silk the color of the clearest waters.

Long, white gloves covered her arms, and a blue band of silk adorned her upswept hair. White pearl earrings and a black velvet choker completed the outfit, along with a pair of delicate glass slippers perfectly molded to her dainty feet.

"It's like a dream!" Cinderella exclaimed, spinning and twirling and admiring her new gown. "A wonderful dream come true!"

Her Fairy Godmother smiled gently. "Yes, my child," she said. "But like all dreams, I'm afraid this can't last forever. You'll have only until midnight and then—"

"Midnight?" Cinderella interrupted happily. Midnight was still hours away. "Oh, thank you!"

"Oh, now, just a minute," her Fairy Godmother said more sternly. "You must understand, my dear, on the stroke of twelve the spell will be broken, and everything will be as it was before."

Cinderella stepped toward her, still smiling. "Oh, I understand," she assured her. "But it's more than I ever hoped for."

The Fairy Godmother relaxed and returned her smile. "Bless you, my child."

It was time to go. Cinderella lifted the hem of her skirt and hurried toward the coach. The footman held the door for her as she climbed inside. The horses snorted and moved off at the command of the coachman. Cinderella barely had time to wave her thanks to her Fairy Godmother before the coach moved off toward the palace. She was on her way!

It wasn't a long trip, and soon the coach was pulling up at the foot of the palace steps. Not even the palace guards, who had already seen the most beautiful and elegant young women in the kingdom pass them that night, could resist a second look at Cinderella in her stunning gown.

She climbed the steps and entered the ballroom.

It was crowded with elegantly dressed people.
Cinderella gazed about in awe, not sure which way
to go first—she had never been inside the palace
before. As she stood there uncertainly, she glanced
up and saw a young man striding toward her.

He stopped before her and bowed. Blushing
slightly, she curtsied in return. She had never seen
such a handsome young man. He was tall and dark

haired, with intelligent eyes and a courteous manner. It was the Prince.

The Prince reached for her hand and kissed it. "May I have this dance, miss?" he asked politely.

"Yes," Cinderella replied.

Cinderella didn't say another word. There was no need. The Prince led her toward the dance floor, and just like that, they were dancing.

The orchestra was playing a waltz. The Prince and Cinderella danced beautifully together as if they'd done so many times before. And indeed, something about the young man made Cinderella feel comfortable—as if they knew each other even without speaking.

Cinderella didn't notice her stepmother and stepsisters staring at her, trying to figure out why the lovely young lady in the elegant gown looked so familiar. She was completely unaware of the many other eyes on her as she danced. She was also completely unaware that the young man was the Prince.

So this is love, she thought with wonder as he

led her out into the palace garden. They continued to dance there, watched only by the stars in the sky overhead.

Finally growing tired, they stopped dancing and walked instead. Hand in hand, they wandered through the darkened gardens and over a footbridge that crossed a small, sparkling stream. They paused in the middle of the bridge, turning toward each other. Cinderella's heart swelled as they embraced.

As their lips touched, a sudden sound broke the silence of the garden.

Bong!

"Oh!" Cinderella cried, pulling back from the young man. "Oh, my goodness!"

"What's the matter?" the Prince asked.

Cinderella glanced at the clock tower as it let out another chime. "It's midnight!" she exclaimed. How could she have lost track of the time? How could she have forgotten her Fairy Godmother's warning?

"Yes, so it is." The young man looked confused. "But why . . . ?"

"Good-bye!" Cinderella cried, pulling away as the clock continued to chime. How many strikes had it been? She had to hurry, or her secret would be revealed! It had been such a perfect evening, and she just wanted to remember it that way.

The young man hurried after her, catching her by the hand. "Oh, no, wait!" he exclaimed. "You can't go now."

"Oh, I must," Cinderella insisted desperately, letting go of his hand. With every chime she grew more frantic. "Please, please, I must!"

"But why?" The Prince couldn't understand why the young woman was suddenly so eager to leave.

There was no time to explain the truth, even if she'd wanted to. She had to come up with a reason—it wasn't fair to let the young man wonder. "W-Well, I," she stammered, trying to think of an excuse. "The Prince! I—I haven't met the Prince!"

"The Prince?" the Prince repeated in surprise. "But didn't you know . . . ?"

The clock chimed again—time was running out!

"Good-bye!" Cinderella cried again, running away at last.

"Wait!" the young man's voice followed her. "Come back! Oh, please, come back! I don't even know your name. How will I find you?"

Cinderella hardly heard him. She didn't dare slow down or even look back. Gathering her skirts, she raced through the ballroom and across the grand entryway to the front steps. Her coach was at the bottom waiting for her. Maybe there was still time. . . .

As she raced down the steps, one of her glass slippers fell off. She paused and turned around to retrieve it, but before she could, she spotted a man in a palace uniform coming after her. "Mademoiselle," he called. "Just a moment!"

Now what? Cinderella

couldn't imagine what he wanted, but there was no time to find out. Leaving the glass slipper behind, she ran the rest of the way down the steps and leaped into her coach.

"Guards!" the man called. "Guards, follow that coach!"

Why were they chasing her? Cinderella had no idea. She didn't realize that the young man she'd spent the evening with was really the Prince, and that he was determined to stop her from rushing away out of his life. All Cinderella knew was that the clock was nearing the last stroke of midnight.

Sure enough, one last *bong* rang out over the

kingdom. And with it, the magic spell ended. The galloping horses changed into running mice. The coachman and footman returned to their ordinary shapes as horse and dog. And Cinderella suddenly found herself sitting atop a pumpkin, wearing her old, ripped pink dress.

There was barely enough time to dash off the road and into hiding in the brush when the King's men galloped by in search of them. Their horses' hooves smashed the pumpkin into smithereens, but Cinderella and her animal friends escaped unhurt and unnoticed.

Finally, when the searchers had passed, Cinderella let out a sigh of relief and turned to her friends. "I'm sorry," she told them. "I—I guess I forgot about everything, even the time. But—but it was so wonderful!" She sighed happily, thinking back over the incredible evening. Her thoughts focused on the young man. She didn't even know his name, but she knew she would never forget him as long as she lived. "And he was so handsome—and then we danced—oh, I'm sure even the Prince himself couldn't have been more—"

Suddenly, one of the mice began chattering and pointing at Cinderella's foot. Looking down, Cinderella gasped in surprise. She was still wearing one of the glass slippers! It hadn't changed back to an ordinary shoe.

Cinderella smiled, guessing that this was a special gift from her Fairy Godmother. Now she would have a memento of this glorious evening. Even if nothing good ever happened to her again, she would always be able to look at this beautiful, perfect glass slipper and remember the most magical night of her life.

"Oh!" she cried, clutching the slipper to her chest. She smiled up at the sky, knowing somehow that her Fairy Godmother would be able to hear her. "Thank you! Thank you so much—for everything!"

THE ROYAL PROCLAMATION

The next morning, a notice was posted in the town square:

Whereas the King desires a search be conducted throughout the kingdom in order to find that certain maiden whose foot shall fit a certain glass slipper; and Whereas said maiden is the one and only true love of our noble Prince, So Be It Proclaimed That, upon finding said maiden, His Royal Highness the Prince will humbly request her hand in marriage to rule with him as Royal Princess and future Queen.

The notice was marked with the official seal of the King. Lady Tremaine saw the posting and realized this could be the chance her daughters needed. She had been outraged that Anastasia and Drizella hadn't had even a moment to talk with and charm the Prince—that strange girl in the pale blue dress had monopolized his company all evening. It was outrageous!

But now, everything could be made right. All she had to do was make sure that one of the girls' feet fit into that slipper. . . .

"Cinderella!" she shouted as she entered the house. "Cinderella! Cinderella! Oh, where is that—"

"Here I am," Cinderella interrupted, appearing in the doorway.

"Oh!" Lady Tremaine was momentarily startled by Cinderella's sudden appearance. And what was that strange faraway expression on her face? But she didn't have time to worry about such things right now. "My daughters," she snapped. "Where are they?"

"I think they're still in bed," Cinderella responded rather dreamily.

Lady Tremaine frowned at her. "Oh," she said. "Oh, well, don't just stand there. Bring up the breakfast trays at once. Hurry!"

As Lady Tremaine rushed up the stairs toward her daughters' bedrooms, Cinderella wandered to the kitchen. She hummed softly while she prepared the break-fast trays. Somehow, even ordi-nary chores didn't seem so bad  this morning. All she had to do was think about the night before and she was filled with happiness.

The only sad part was knowing she would probably never see that young man again. But she couldn't possibly complain about that. Just meeting him, spending that one glorious evening dancing with him, had been a dream come true. How could she ask for more than that?

Lifting the heavy trays, she headed upstairs, still

humming. She headed for Anastasia's bedroom, but even before she reached it, she could hear her stepmother talking to her daughters inside.

"Hurry now," she was exclaiming, her stern voice sounding excited. "He'll be here any minute!"

"Who will?" Drizella was standing in the doorway of her sister's room, looking sleepy.

"The Grand Duke!" Lady Tremaine responded impatiently. "He's been hunting all night for that girl."

Cinderella paused in the hallway, wondering what her stepmother was talking about.

"The one who lost her slipper at the ball last night," Lady Tremaine went on. "They say he's madly in love with her!"

"The Duke is?" Anastasia asked in confusion.

"No, no, no!" her mother exclaimed. "The Prince!"

Cinderella gasped. "The Prince!" she whispered. Suddenly, everything made sense. That handsome young man—the palace official chasing her—and now this.

Her whole body seemed to go numb. The Prince! In love with her! One of the breakfast trays slipped out of her hands and crashed to the floor.

The sudden noise attracted Lady Tremaine's attention. She glared at Cinderella. "You clumsy little fool. Clean that up, and then help my daughters dress."

"What for?" Drizella complained sourly.

Anastasia nodded. "If he's in love with that girl, why should we even bother?"

"Now you two listen to me," Lady Tremaine replied sharply. "There is still a chance that one of you can get him. No one—not even the Prince—knows who that girl is. The glass slipper is their only clue. The Duke has been ordered to try it on every girl in the kingdom, and if one can be found whom the slipper fits, then by the King's command, that girl shall be the Prince's bride."

Cinderella was listening as she cleaned up the fallen tray. She sat up straight in awe. "His bride," she whispered. It was such an amazing thought that she hardly dared to think it. That wonderful young man—the Prince!—wanted her to be his bride!

She was hardly aware that her stepsisters were gathering up their best clothes and piling them in her arms to launder and mend. She stared into space, still trying to take in the shock of this news. The Prince! She was in love with the Prince!

And he was in love with her!

Without realizing what she was doing, she let everything drop to the floor and, deaf to her stepsisters' protests, wandered off down the hall. She wanted to wash up before the Duke arrived. As she climbed the stairs toward her own room, she was still humming the chorus of a waltz she had danced to the night before.

Meanwhile Lady Tremaine was staring at her suspiciously.

"What's the matter with her?" Anastasia complained.

"Mother, did you see what she did?" Drizella added. "Why, I never saw—"

"Quiet!" her mother commanded. Recognizing the tune that Cinderella was humming, Lady Tremaine realized that her stepdaughter must have been at the ball. So that was why that lovely young lady had seemed so familiar last night. . . . She had no idea how Cinderella had done it, but she didn't plan to let her get away with it.

Leaving her daughters behind to gather up their clothes, Lady Tremaine crept up the stairs after Cinderella. When she reached the tower, she could hear the girl still humming and singing in her room. Her eyes narrowed as she watched her from the doorway.

Cinderella brushed her hair. As she gazed into the mirror, she caught a glimpse of her stepmother.

Lady Tremaine reached around the door and
took the key from the lock. Before Cinderella could
stop her, she slammed the door shut—and locked it
from the outside!

"No!" Cinderella cried, spinning around and racing for the door. "Please, you can't—you can't!"

But she had. The door was locked tight.

"Let me out!" Cinderella cried. Her words
turned into sobs as she realized what was

going on. Her stepmother meant to keep her locked up in the tower until the Duke had come and gone. She felt her dreams slipping away once again. "Let me out! You must let me out!"

The mice had seen the whole thing. Once again, they went to the aid of their dear friend Cinderella. . . .

The mice scurried downstairs through the walls. The key was in Lady Tremaine's pocket. Could they steal it back and free Cinderella? There wasn't much time—already the Duke's carriage was pulling up in front of the house.

In the parlor, Lady Tremaine felt very pleased with herself. That had been a close one—Cinderella had nearly ruined all her plans. But now it was just a matter of forcing that glass slipper onto one of her daughters' feet, and their future would be secured.

"Now remember," she warned her daughters as she got ready to open the door and admit the Duke, "this is your last chance. Don't fail me!"

Soon the Duke was calling for the glass slipper, which a footman brought to him, nestled on a silk pillow. He wasn't sure why he bothered—he had seen the lovely young woman the Prince was speaking to, and she had looked nothing at all like these two girls. Still, he had his orders—he was to try the slipper on every maiden's foot.

"Why, that's my slipper!" Drizella cried, reaching for it.

Anastasia pushed her aside. "It's my slipper!" she exclaimed.

"Girls! Girls! Your manners!" Lady Tremaine cried. She smiled at the Duke. "A thousand pardons, Your Grace." She was so busy imagining the grand life the three of them would soon be leading at the palace that she didn't notice when the mice formed a chain and lifted the key right out of her pocket!

The Duke read the proclamation, then announced that it was time to proceed with the fitting. He held out the slipper as Anastasia extended her large, knobby foot.

"There!" Anastasia cried, hoping against hope that the Duke wouldn't notice that the tiny slipper was dangling off her big toe. "I knew it was my slipper." She grimaced as the Duke gave her a skeptical look. "Oh, well, it may be a trifle snug today. You know how it is— dancing all night."

She struggled to shove the rest of her foot into the slipper, but it was no use. The slipper was much too small.

Then it was Drizella's turn. But her foot was no smaller or daintier than her sister's. She puffed and panted and labored to squeeze her foot into the slipper, but it was no use.

The Duke grabbed the slipper back before Drizella could damage it. He stood, preparing to move on to the next house.

"You are the only ladies of the household, I hope?" He corrected the slip of the tongue quickly. "I presume?"

Lady Tremaine's face was grim. "There's no one else, Your Grace."

"Quite so." The Duke put on his hat and turned toward the door. "Good day."

"Your Grace!" a new voice stopped him. "Your Grace!"

Cinderella raced down the stairs. The mice had  done it—they had released her from her tower prison just in the nick of time!

"Please, wait!" Cinderella cried. "May I try it on?"

The Duke removed his hat again, stunned by the beauty of the simply dressed young girl hurrying toward him. Meanwhile, Lady Tremaine and her daughters were chattering their protests:

"Pay no attention to her. . . ."

"It's only Cinderella . . . our scullery maid. . . ."

But the Duke ignored them. He smiled at Cinderella, holding out his hand as she reached the bottom of the stairs.

"Come, my child," he told her kindly. He led her to a chair and gestured for the footman to bring the slipper.

But as the footman hurried toward him, Lady Tremaine made one last desperate attempt to foil Cinderella. She stuck out her walking stick and tripped the footman. He lurched forward, and the slipper flew off its pillow. It sailed through the air—and shattered into a thousand pieces against the hard marble floor.

The Duke gasped in horror. "Oh, no, no, no!" he cried, flinging himself to the ground and picking up the broken pieces. Now what would he do? Could he possibly put the slipper together again? "This is terrible," he moaned. "The King—what will he say? What will he do?"

Cinderella was still sitting in her chair. "Perhaps if it would help . . ." she began.

The Duke was still kneeling before the broken slipper. "No, no, nothing can help now, nothing!" he wailed.

Cinderella brought something out of her pocket and held it up. "But you see," she said, "I have the other slipper."

Both Lady Tremaine and the Duke froze in

shock—one horrified, one jubilant. The Duke was
the first to react.

He smiled and rushed toward the girl, grabbing the
second glass slipper and kissing it with relief. Then,
before anything else could happen, he
carefully slid the slipper onto the
girl's dainty foot.

It fit perfectly, as he had
known it would.

A Dream Come True

Cinderella smiled at her reflection in the mirror. She could hardly believe that she was here in the palace, and that it was her wedding day. In just a few moments, she would be standing beside her true love—the Prince—and they would declare their eternal devotion to each other in front of the whole kingdom. It seemed almost too good to be true!

"Thank you," she said to the servants who were adjusting her veil. "Thank you so much!"

She stared again at her reflection. Her wedding

gown was beautiful—pure white, with long sleeves
and a full, sweeping skirt. Around her throat she
wore a slim black velvet ribbon just like the one she'd
worn the night she'd met her Prince.

At that moment, her Fairy Godmother appeared
beside her in the mirror. Her eyes were
twinkling.

"Oh!" Cinderella cried, turning to hug her. "I
was hoping you would come!"

"I wouldn't miss it for the world, child," her Fairy Godmother responded, squeezing her tightly. "You look marvelous! Simply beautiful."

"Thank you." Cinderella blushed. "Thank you for everything. I never dreamed anything so wonderful could ever happen to me."

Her Fairy Godmother winked. "Of course you did, my dear." She explained: "You've had your troubles—more than most people, I'd say—but through it all you never lost faith that things would get better. You never stopped believing in the future. That's the only way to find happiness, you know."

Cinderella smiled, realizing that her Fairy Godmother was right. Deep within her heart, she had kept right on wishing and dreaming and hoping, even when things looked their darkest.

Soon, a servant knocked on the door. The ceremony was about to begin. The Fairy Godmother disappeared as the other woman entered, but

Cinderella knew her Fairy Godmother would be watching from wherever she was.

The servant looked at the future princess and smiled. In her short time in the palace, Cinderella had already won the hearts of the entire staff with her pleasant and humble manner.

"Dear girl," the woman said kindly, "you are the most beautiful bride I have seen in all my seventy years. I hope you will also be the happiest."

"Thank you," Cinderella responded shyly. She knew the old woman's wish had already come true. No one could possibly be any happier than Cinderella was at this moment!

As she walked down the aisle a few minutes later, Cinderella saw many familiar faces in the crowd. The King was there, of course, beaming with pride at his handsome son and future daughter-in-law.

The Grand Duke and other officials were there as well.

Cinderella even spotted Gus and the other mice cheering her on, dressed up in tiny blue coats for the special occasion. She smiled at them, knowing that they were enjoying palace life just as much as she was. Not only were there much nicer scraps to steal from the palace kitchen but the mice no longer had to worry about escaping Lucifer's claws!

Thinking of the grumpy old cat reminded Cinderella of her stepfamily. She glanced around, but Lady Tremaine and her daughters were nowhere to be seen in the crowd. Cinderella felt a brief touch of regret. Her stepfamily still refused to accept her good fortune and share in her happiness. Cinderella had sent the Duke to their château with an invitation to the wedding. Even after all their years of

petty cruelty, she was willing to make amends. But clearly, her stepfamily had been unable to accept her kindness.

Still, Cinderella wouldn't let such thoughts dampen her joy on this wonderful day. All she could do was see that her stepfamily had enough money to get by from now on. The rest was up to them. They would have to find their own happiness, just as she had.

The ceremony flew by all too quickly. Soon, Cinderella found herself running down the steps, hand in hand with her new husband. Halfway down, one of her slippers fell off. Laughing, she paused to retrieve it. The Prince laughed, too, then led her the rest of the way down the stairs. At the bottom, a grand carriage was waiting to whisk them away on their honeymoon.

The entire kingdom had gathered outside the palace to see the happy royal couple. There were shouts of congratulations and cheers from all sides. Cinderella did her best to wave her thanks to every-